Good-bye TO THE Trees

by Vicky Shiefman

Atheneum 1993 New York

MAXWELL MACMILLAN CANADA
TORONTO
MAXWELL MACMILLAN INTERNATIONAL
NEW YORK   OXFORD   SINGAPORE   SYDNEY

Atheneum   Maxwell Macmillan Canada, Inc.
Macmillan Publishing Company   1200 Eglinton Avenue East
866 Third Avenue   Suite 200
New York, NY 10022   Don Mills, Ontario M3C 3N1

Macmillan Publishing Company is part of the
Maxwell Communication Group of Companies.

First edition
Printed in the United States of America
10 9 8 7 6 5 4 3 2 1
The text of this book is set in 12 pt. Garamond Book.
Book design by Kimberly M. Adlerman

Shiefman, Vicky.
Good-bye to the trees / Vicky Shiefman. —1st ed.
p.   cm.
Summary: Despite the excitement and confusion of her new life in
America, thirteen-year-old Fagel can't forget the family she left behind in
Russia.
ISBN 0–689–31806–5
[1. Emigration and immigration—Fiction.   2. Russian Americans—
Fiction.   3. Jews—Fiction.]   I. Title.
PZ7.S5547Go   1993
[Fic]—dc20   92–22260

In memory of my grandmother,
Fagel Fratrizsky Goldman Winokur,
1894–1987,
and my father, Saul Shiefman,
1917–1987.
And dedicated to my brother, Joe

THANKS TO SUE ALEXANDER,
MIRIAM COHEN,
GAIL PARIS,
EMMA SHIEFMAN,
AND THE LATE ANN TROY.

GRATEFUL ACKNOWLEDGMENT
FOR THEIR EXPERTISE
REGARDING THE HISTORICAL ELEMENTS
OF MY STORY
DR. LUCJAN DOBROSZYCKI
HARRIET DAVIS-KRAM

_C_HAPTER _1_

Mother tried to warn me the day before I left our little town in Russia. That day, she took me into the woods, just the two of us. It was July 26, 1907. I will never forget.

Blume and Nahamkah were in the kitchen when we left and they begged to join us. I was surprised when Mother said no. I thought it must be very important if just Mother and I were going.

It was.

Mother and I left our mill house and walked along the bank of the Szczara, not talking, for quite a while. We passed the summer flowers, the little fruit trees, the weeping willows. (They're my favorites because they seem most alive. Willows don't just stand still like the other trees. Whenever the winds blow, their full branches cluster together and really sway.) Deeper and deeper we went into the woods until we found my favorite log, the one I like to sit on when I need to be by myself and think. When we arrived there, I asked Mother to sit down.

Then she said something which made me sad:

"Say good-bye to the trees, you may never see them again."

I shivered. It sounded so final.

"What do you mean?" I asked her for reassurance.

"America is very far away," she explained. "You can't just come back and forth the way Hatzkel does from his watchmaking trade in Bialystok. I don't know when we will see you again so now is the time to say good-bye."

"But, Mother, I thought I was going so I could save up money and send for you and the family. Otherwise I wouldn't go."

"Yes, Fagel, dear, you're right. But we never know what the future may bring. Only God does. Right now if your father, may he rest in peace, were here, you wouldn't be going without us. Still, you're lucky because your father's brother can take you—that is, if you want to go now."

"But, of course I want to go. I mean I want to go first, to get everything ready so you can join me."

"Yes," said Mother, "but Fagel, dear, if it is too

2

difficult for you to go alone, you don't have to. You're only thirteen, and I'm not sure I should be sending you, even if you're going to stay with my brother and his family in Boston."

"But Mamenyu, my little Mommy, I'm not a little girl."

"You feel that way now," said Mother. "It's an adventure, new, exciting, but you could change your mind. You don't know what it's like to live without your family."

That's true, I thought to myself.

Then Mother spoke again.

"But Fagel, if you want to, you can always come back to Slonim—no matter where you are, no matter what else is happening. I will find the money. If necessary, I will even come get you."

"Mamenyu," I pleaded, "you won't have to get me."

"No," she said, reading my feelings better than my words. "There's nothing to be ashamed of. Uncle who is taking you came back. My brother's family, who you are going to in Boston, went with my parents and other brothers and their families to Argentina and didn't like it there. So they came back here before they went to the United States. Do you remember when they stayed with us?"

I nodded yes, though it was vague in my mind.

"Ten years ago it was. Itkeh was about five. She's older than you. Libeh was three, the same age as you. Then the twins were born. Remember? We didn't have enough mattresses so we wrapped them in cloth and put them on hay in the barn." She laughed. "But they did fine and now there are more children.

"So, little Fagel-bird, the Lishofskys came back and went off again. So did Uncle. You can too. Understand?"

"Yes, Mamenyu."

She stopped, looked at me, and put her arm around me.

"Poor little Fagel," she said as she drew me close.

For a minute, maybe more, I wanted to be as little a girl as she made me feel. I wanted to crawl into her lap and pretend I was a baby.

"If only your father were here," she continued.

Tears started to fill her eyes but she wiped them away with her apron.

"Mamenyu," I said, "don't worry. Everything will be fine. You'll see. Soon we'll all be together again."

"God willing," said Mother.

For a while we huddled in each other's warmth on that day in the woods. I wished it would have gone on forever. I wished she could have come with me on this trip . . . and more . . . so many wishes.

All too soon, Mother stood up and regained her usual role.

"Tonight we will be preparing a farewell dinner so don't come to the kitchen. I want it to be a surprise. Now I've got to go get everything ready."

"Yes, Mamenyu."

She walked off in the direction of the mill. I ran and caught up to her for another hug. I didn't want to let her go! Finally, I did let go and watched her make her way back to the house. She was such a brave little Mamenyu.

When she was out of sight, I decided to visit my special trees, the ones that reminded me of the family.

First I found the little mulberry, just starting to grow. I called this sweet little tree Herschel. Before putting one of its long, purplish red fruits in my mouth, I said, to myself, "Good-bye, Herschel."

Next, I went deeper into the woods to find the tree I named after Pinchas. The straight, blue-green tamarack was so upright, it could have been a pole. Its cones pointed up too, just like my God-fearing brother. As I touched its bark, I whispered, "Good-bye, Pinchas."

Nearby was the pine I called Zelig because its cones curved back toward the branches, something silly just like Zelig was. I pulled one off and touched its prickles. They stung, like one of Zelig's bad jokes.

"Good-bye, Zelig," I murmured, blinking back tears.

When I found the black cherry that I named for Blume, I threw my arms around it. As long as I held on, I didn't need to cry. At the end of the hug, I stepped back to look at its beauty—the long, white flowers, dark purple fruit, and evenly spaced branches.

"Good-bye, Blume," I said aloud.

I walked quietly to the flowering dogwood or Nahamkah. Down I sat on the ground, watching little animals and birds eat its clusters of red fruits. How delicate were its thin trunk and slender branches. After what seemed a long time, I said, "Good-bye, Nahamkah."

Slowly I made my way to my black spruce and, with both hands, held onto its lowest branch. It seemed to offer the same comfort as my tall, oldest brother. I didn't need to look at my Hatzkel tree, just feel its strength. Eventually I was ready to say "Good-bye, Hatzkel."

Then I visited the linden with heart-shaped leaves and smells like honey. Its full leaves and flowered branches sheltered me as Mother did. I would have liked to stay forever but I didn't. Instead, I said loudly and clearly, "Good-bye, Mamenyu."

Next it was time to visit the majestic white oak tree. With its strong trunk and branches, it was the tree that reminded me of Daddy. I scrambled up to the bottom branch and surveyed my woods. I hated leaving them. I only hoped my decision to go to America was right. But there was nothing more to do or say. I climbed down, hugged the oak trunk, and said aloud, "Good-bye, Daddy."

On the way back, I stopped in the women's bath-house, took off everything but my underwear, put my feet in the water, and splashed nice, cool river wetness on my face and hands. When I finished, I walked to our mill house, humming "Raizele."

"On a quiet street,
In a little house,
There in an attic,
My Raizele lives.
Under her window,
I linger at night,
Whistle, and then call,
'Come out, dear, come out!' "

Back home I packed for my trip and began to dream a little. Who knows, maybe I will find a boy in America who will call me to come out. Who knows? There, anything is possible.

Nahamkah came into the room and sat on the boys' bed to watch me. My suitcase was resting on the girls' bed, ours.

"Fagel," she said, "why are you so happy? Are you glad to be leaving us?"

She looked upset.

"Silly," I told her. "Until you join me, I'll miss you all the time. After all, who else would bump me at night?"

"You never can tell—someone else, maybe a husband."

"Aii, Nahamkah," I screamed, pretending to hit

her. "What are you saying! Watch me pack and make sure I'm not forgetting anything."

She watched me open the dresser drawer. There wasn't much to take: a few shirts, two skirts, one dress, some underwear, a few hankies. I folded them carefully and put them in the trunk Mother had given me.

"What else should I take?" I asked her. "I can't think of anything. Can you?"

"No," she said solemnly, staring at me as I moved about.

I stopped.

"What is it, Nahamkah? What do you want to say?"

"I have something for you, Fagel."

She went to her dresser drawer and took out a picture.

"Here. I want you to take this."

I looked at the picture; it was the whole family—Father, Mother, her, me, Blume, and the boys, when we were little. Even then Zelig wore his crooked smile and Pinchas looked serious like a good Talmud student. Blume was as sturdy as a tree trunk and Nahamkah was propped up between Blume and me, in case she fell. Mother looked less sad than now but just as strong, and Father, may he rest in peace, was not only healthy, but handsome. I stared at it awhile. It made me think how much we had grown. I felt like a young woman now. There, in the picture, maybe I was nine, just a girl. So were my younger sisters. Herschel was a baby. And I had forgotten how handsome Father was. It made me realize that we would never be all together again. Though it was a lovely picture, it made me sad.

I hate to keep sad things around.

"I can't take that," I told Nahamkah.

"Why not?" she said, looking hurt. "I want to give you something before you go. I want you to think of us and always love us."

I sat down next to her on the bed and put my arm around her. "Nahamkah, how could I not think of you? You are my sister and this is my family. You are the only family I have."

She put her hand in mine.

"Remember when baby Herschel missed our father so much, he took a spoon and tried to scrape out the dirt between the floorboards? Poor little boy. He thought he would find our father in the earth. Will you miss me that much?"

She looked like she was going to cry.

I couldn't stand it. I've had enough crying to last a lifetime. But I couldn't say this to Nahamkah. Instead I asked, "Where did you get this picture?"

"Mother gave it to me."

"But it's a family picture," I told her. "I couldn't take it from the house."

"No, it's mine," Nahamkah said, "I looked at it and looked at it and kept asking Mamenyu to give it to me until one day she said, 'If you love it so much, you should have it.'

"So now it's mine and I want you to have it. I

have nothing else as nice to give you. Please, Fagel, take it. Please. Please have something nice to remember us with."

When I looked at her, I realized she meant it. I knew the picture meant more to her than it did to me or anyone else in the family.

"Are you sure?" I asked her again.

"Please," she repeated.

"All right," I said, and put it under some clothes.

Will the Lishofskys have as sweet a girl as Nahamkah? What will it be like not to have a big brother or even little ones?

*C*HAPTER *2*

This boat, the *Barbarossa*, is dreadful. But I can stand it because I'm going to the New World. Uncle warned me before we boarded; yet I couldn't have imagined what it smells like! There are rows of endless beds and people who fill each one and more. When they get sick from the rocking of the boat, where can they go? We have no place to wash our clothes or ourselves. We smell like garbage.

Of course, it's never quiet. It's not just the babies and little children who cry. The older people yell or have family fights and groan or make noises in their sleep. I think of all the talking in my family and multiply that by too many families living in one big room. It's always too noisy.

That's down below where we sleep. It's better on deck where they serve us what they call food (herring and black bread that's as hard as a rock).

On deck, the air cleans me and I can watch the waves. The water reminds me of our own Szczara River and home. The ocean has only one problem— it goes on forever. At home, you always saw the other bank of the Szczara. Here all you see is water and more water so I don't like to look out too far. It's scary to think we're in the middle of a big nowhere.

Those little round windows called portholes are just a piece of glass. What would happen if one should open and all that water came rushing in? Why, we'd drown, that's what. So I don't like to think about too much water, just enough to think we're moving closer to America all the time.

I am very grateful that Uncle is taking me. He has been very good. When he sees me frown, he says, "Don't worry, the boat will get us there, the government won't hurt you." Since he's been back and forth three times already, he knows exactly what to expect.

When our train arrived at Bremen we weren't allowed to board the boat until the next day so we stayed at the home of people he knew. They used to sell machinery for mills, just like Grandma and

Grandpa in Slonim! They gave us a delicious dinner—kugel noodle pudding, meat, fruit.

Also, before boarding there were some examinations.

The doctor put sticks in my hair, eyes, mouth, and a needle—a big, long metal one—in my arm. That hurt! I had to wash my body in a room filled with women and children I'd never seen before. The woman directing us travelers rushed us. Quickly I took my clothes off, folded them in a pile on top of my trunk, and hurried under these metal things on the wall that dripped out water. Strangers were looking at me naked! I can only guess what color my body looked, blue from the cold or red from the embarrassment. Even my face felt flushed.

After the physical, the mental examination began. The inspector looked at my ticket and papers and asked: How old are you? Where do you come from? Are you married? What's your work? Who are you traveling with? Have you had any childhood diseases?

When the questions ended, I was finally free to board. I was glad!

Sometimes I even have fun here.

A whole group of people sit up on deck and sing.

Next to them sit the same women who've stayed together for most of the trip. They're just like the "Sabbath women," the gossips outside of the synagogue, who tell stories about everyone and then spit three times so the evil eye won't get them.

I joined the singers. We even sang my favorite, "Raizele."

I noticed one woman with sad eyes who kept silent.

I asked one of the singers, "What is the matter with that lady? She never sings."

"She doesn't sing?" my friend answered loudly. "She doesn't talk. We're lucky she stands up and puts food in her mouth. After what happened to her, you'd be lucky to be alive."

"What happened?"

"Don't ask. You wouldn't want to know."

I looked at the lady. She was rocking back and forth.

Then my friend began.

"It was horrible. I didn't see but they told me about it. With God's help, I was out of town. When I came back, it wasn't even the same village I lived in. They had burned down whole rows of houses. And that, little lady, was the best part.

"The worst I can't even say. Not even I can speak of the horrors of a pogrom—what it does to people!"

She shook her head.

"Look at her. You can see.

"First they burnt her house down. Her husband was inside.

"With the baby in her arms she ran away. She kept running and running until she came to a field but it didn't do any good because some of them were on horses. They always are. It wasn't just drunken peasants, you understand, but officers on their horses. They all love to torture us Jews.

"She found a ditch in this field, jumped into it, and wrapped the baby in her arms. She rocked the baby back and forth to keep him quiet so they wouldn't find her.

"The baby was so quiet she wondered if he was alive.

"He was. The baby gave one loud piercing scream.

"The officers found her, ripped the baby from her arms, threw him in the air like he was a ball...

"Then he *was* dead.

"What they did to her afterward no one knows.

"The other Jewish towns did what they could. As soon as they heard, they sent us food and clothing and money. Our community leaders bought tickets for the families that were hurt the most.

"I lost seven—my sister, brother-in-law, their children, and a great aunt—but then I had a big family, especially when you're counting all my mother and father's relatives."

I put my hand to my heart, almost as if to check that it was still beating.

"I told you not to ask."

"I'm so sorry," I said.

"Sorry?" she laughed bitterly. "You didn't do it. *They* should be sorry!"

I turned away and walked to the side of the ship. If I felt sick, I could always lean over.

Then I saw the waves. Their endlessness did not scare me anymore. Their roar and strength and majesty comforted me. The waves were bringing me to the New World, just as I would bring my family, all of them, away from the horrors of the old.

CHAPTER 3

Well, I finally landed. I'm off the boat. But I'm not in Boston yet. I'm on a little island off the United States of America called Ellis. It's where Americans check us immigrants to see if we're good enough to live in their country. So far I'm not good enough.

I don't understand it. Everything's too confusing.

The *Barbarossa* came to a stop. We got into other little boats that brought us here. All this time, Uncle was at my side. When we got to Ellis Island, none of the cousins was there to meet me. Instead, Uncle and I stood in these long lines where they check your hair, skin, scalp—all the same things they did in Europe. Physically I was fine but when I got in line where they asked questions, I was in trouble. By that time, Uncle had left for Milwaukee.

"Don't worry," he said before he left, "American people are good, even government people."

When it came my turn, an inspector spoke to me alone.

"Do you have any money on you, Fagel?" he asked with a crooked smile.

I showed him the twenty-five dollars mother had given me.

"Imagine you traveled all the way here by yourself!"

I bowed my head.

"Actually my uncle from Milwaukee brought me."

"Is he with you now?"

"No," I had to admit, "he hurried back to earn the money to bring his family over."

"So you're alone?"

I nodded yes.

"And you, Fagel, how do you plan to support yourself in the United States of America?"

"As a dressmaker."

"Where?"

"In Boston."

"Do you have a job there?"

"Not yet."

"Are you a good dressmaker?"

"Yes. I studied for three years with Mr. Antowicki.

I can even make buttonholes. Long ago I learned the easy things like hems, cutting patterns, sewing on buttons, and putting pieces together. I can even work the machine—"

He interrupted me, "But how will you survive until you get a job?"

"I'm going to stay with my cousins, the Lishofskys."

"Are they here?"

"I don't know. Where would they be? Is there a special place where families meet? My uncle didn't tell me."

"Yes, Fagel, and if they had been here, we would have known, so we can assume they're not."

"Oh," I said, trying not to sound as disappointed as I felt.

"Where do the Lishofskys live?"

I took out a letter that they had written to Mother with their address in the corner, and handed it to him.

He smiled that funny smile again.

"Did your cousins know you were coming?"

"Yes. Of course. I wouldn't have come unless they asked me to."

"Yes, Fagel, but did they know if you were coming today?"

"I don't know," I had to admit. "My mother is the one who writes to them and then tells me what to do."

"Can you write too?"

"Certainly. The university graduates taught me to read and write a nice Yiddish, just like you speak."

This time I looked straight at him, not away.

"Well, Fagel, your cousins might not know that you've arrived."

He left his desk, stood next to me, and whispered, "Don't worry. I'll fix everything up. I'll write them now and they'll be here soon. It'll only cost five dollars."

I looked up at him in surprise.

"Quickly," he said, "the money."

I put it in his hand and he moved smoothly back to his desk.

"Now sit down on a chair and wait until a matron takes you to our dormitory," he directed loudly.

I felt like I was going to collapse. I could barely drag myself over to the nearby chair where he told me to wait. Next to me were women with children draped around them, crying and muttering to themselves. I stared into the distance. I can't tell for how long or what I was looking at. I couldn't believe it. No one was there to meet me and they weren't letting me into the real United States.

Even when Uncle left, I hadn't cried. Instead, I thanked him for bringing me over. I was strong and brave, like Mother, but sitting in that chair with all the moaning and "woe-is-me's," I couldn't help it. I joined the chorus of tears, the symphony of self-pity.

20

Then a girl about my age got up and stood next to me.

"Don't cry," she said, "I know it's terrible to be alone here but someone will come soon. I know."

She was Sarah, a fourteen-year-old Jewish girl from Romania. She was tall and had blond, curly hair that framed her square-shaped face.

That evening, she and I slept in adjoining bunk beds in the crowded dormitory.

I had a good time with Sarah here. She helped prepare me (as I did her) for what would happen if she should leave before I did or I before her. We decided not to spend time with people who tell and retell their sad stories but find other things to do.

Sarah's parents came the next morning. I cried when I saw how much they hugged and kissed each other. Then she made me promise not to worry because if good things can happen to her, they can happen to me too.

I hope she's right.

CHAPTER 4

I'm so alone and I don't know if things will get any better. It's been over two weeks and I'm still here on this island.

What will happen if nobody comes for me?

Maybe they will send me back to Europe! That is, to Bremen. What will I do there? The only people I know in Bremen are the Slonimers whose home Uncle and I stayed at. I don't even know what street it's on or remember their last names. How would I ever get back to our family?

So I try not to think too much and find ways to

amuse myself. I count my cash a lot so I can learn its value.

American money is funny. The paper notes have pictures of odd-looking men on the one-, five-, and ten-dollar bills. I prefer coins, so as soon as I could change the bills, I did. Coins are better because they're heavier and clang when you carry them. The funniest is what they call the nickel. It is worth five cents or half as much as the next, the dime, but the dime is a little silver thing while the nickel is bigger and dark-colored. Isn't that silly? Anyway, I like to have nickels ringing in my pocket. Then I visit the store where they sell us detainees little items.

With one nickel I bought an orange. Here an orange is for every day, not just special occasions.

They don't charge for meals and we can eat three times a day! We eat well—thick soups and stews, boiled vegetables, fruits, bread. The spacious dining room in which they serve us is really quite beautiful with its high ceilings.

Also there is a pipe coming out of the wall which you turn off and on. You can take as much water as you want. I can wash every day. I even got a chance to wash my clothes.

If you didn't know where you were, you could pretend you were on vacation at a spa or in a hotel for travelers.

But I know where I am—nowhere. I'm not in the

United States of America, not on the boat, not in Europe. I'm nowhere.

This Ellis Island fools you. The main building where they check you in looks like a castle from the outside. Surrounded by trees and water, it is a handsome, redbrick building with fancy trim and huge towers. How could you guess that inside people are being examined to see if they're good or not, like they did to me?

Sometimes I wander into the balcony, watch the arrivals, and sing "Raizele" to comfort me.

The people look scared but well-dressed, because they're trying to impress the inspectors. I like to see all the different kinds of clothing. I've seen so many kinds of scarves—black, white, different colors, and prints. My favorite was a colorful print worn by a pretty lady with a dark face and a bit of hair showing on the sides. Her scarf was all tucked in and tied on top, as if it were a round cap, very flattering.

I can't believe all the hats. Most men's hats are dark but I know our Blume could recognize all the differences—narrow or wide brims, lying flat or turned up, different ribbons, indented or rounded centers, high or low crowns.

The women's hats have even more materials— straw, felt, heavy brocade. They can be plain or trimmed with ribbons or flowers. The best one looked like a bird made its nest in it.

If only I knew how to read costumes better, I

could tell exactly where everyone in the clothing parade came from.

But not only do I not know where people come from or when or if I can leave this island, I really know little at all. What I really know is, I am alone. I've never been so alone in my life. Even at home, when I'm in the woods by myself or on my way to Antowicki's, after I dropped off Blume at her hat-making class, I'm not alone. I can always find a family member or someone else I know. On the train and boat, I was with Uncle. Then there was Sarah. Now all I see are the woe-is-me people, crying, whining, complaining, and I am catching their disease. When will things change? What can I do? What did I do to deserve this?

I can't shake it. I leave the building where we sleep and go outside to see the beautiful Statue of Liberty. She holds no hope for me. Looking at New York City with its tall buildings just across the water I can't go to, I begin to sob.

I can't stop thinking about the day I left Slonim. Little did I know then what it would be like now. I never could have walked away from the family without crying as I did that day. I thought it was so simple, going in one straight line to America, land of the free and safe.

Nahamkah cried. Mother wiped her eyes with her apron. Blume hugged me so tightly, I almost got scared. Pinchas advised me to help out the family in Boston. Zelig told me to send for him first and together we could start a business and take care of the family in style. Herschel jumped up and down, screaming, *"Fagel, Fagel, Fagel."* I kissed everyone and then turned around to walk to the railroad station with Uncle and the grandparents.

At the time, I remember feeling happy. I was going forward to greet the new. I couldn't understand why everyone was crying. I only turned back once to wave, and Blume had her arm around Nahamkah. Mother clutched that apron tightly in one hand. Zelig and Pinchas, both at the same time, were touching Herschel.

Then I guessed they were crying to be left behind in the sad Old World. Now I wonder. Were they crying for me too? Did they realize how hard it would be to travel so far, so alone?

CHAPTER 5

Tomorrow a lady will arrive to take you to Boston, Fagel," the Yiddish-speaking officer said.

"What lady? What about my cousins?"

"We finally got a letter from them. They don't have the money to come but they are sending a woman they know to get you."

"Thank you," I said, not happy with his answer.

I was disappointed that the cousins weren't coming. I wondered why. Who could I trust?

The next morning I got up early and was already

packed when the lady, dressed in a black, well-cut suit, came for me.

"Fagel," she said in elegant tones that matched her clothes, "you don't know me, but the Lishofskys are my friends. I live on the same street they do, and when they heard I was coming to New York, they asked me to pick you up."

"Thank you," I said.

"Now go get your bag. We're going to take the overnight ferry to Boston."

She looked more American than Jewish, but it didn't matter because she seemed nice. Maybe I could trust her whether she was Jewish or not. I followed her and went to wait at the dock for the little boat. How happy I was to board and be traveling again.

New York City faded into the background. We passed open land, trees, and fewer buildings. I never would have guessed that New York was so far from Boston. We rode that boat for a long time. America must be a very big country. What about all the other places people talk about besides New York and Boston—Milwaukee, Ohio, Minneapolis. I wonder where they are?

The nice lady stayed right beside me the whole way. She even gave me a packed lunch—sandwich, juice, and a fruit. It was the oddest fruit I'd ever seen—yellow with a hard skin and shaped like a half-moon. The lady told me its name was *banana*—

what a funny name, banana. Then she pointed to the towns we were passing and told me their English names. I'd repeat the word after her but I don't know if I got it right. I'm hoping that the same way I remember tunes will help me learn English words. I longed to know everything, just everything, about America. I hoped that Libeh and Itkeh weren't so American they wouldn't speak Yiddish. I also hoped that even if they didn't meet my boat, they would be nice when I got there.

The next day, the boat slowed down. We pulled into Boston Harbor, where my feet finally touched American mainland.

"Now we head for Chelsea," said the lady.

"What's that?" I asked.

"Chelsea is the small town next to Boston, where your cousins live."

"Oh, I thought it was Boston."

"Well, Chelsea is almost Boston."

The lady led me along the street until we found a long car with wires on top. After riding this car for half an hour, we got off and walked some more.

She stopped at one three-storied house and we began to climb stairs. At the third floor, she knocked on the door. A man I'd never seen before opened it. He didn't look like anyone in our family but he didn't seem dangerous, either. So I listened as he spoke first to the lady, then to me.

"Come on, greenhorn. We're expecting you."

The lady turned to me, put one hand on my shoulder and smiled. I shook her hand and said, "Thank you."

Suddenly she disappeared, as if by the same magic that had brought her. Too bad. I guess she had to get back to her own family. I was left with this man who seemed to know me.

"Fagel," he said, "don't be afraid. I am your aunt's brother. Come, everyone is waiting for you."

He carried my trunk into the kitchen where a large group had assembled.

"Here's another mouth to feed," he said, with a wink.

A woman laughed.

"Hello," she said, "I'm your aunt. Remember me?"

I nodded. Her shapeless cotton housedress covered a body heavy with child; she did look like what I remembered of my aunt. I wondered why my introduction began with "another mouth to feed." This was not a good sign.

Everyone began to shout in Yiddish that I had finally arrived.

It was nice to recognize people I had once known in Slonim. Itkeh and Libeh had exactly the same long faces with long noses as when they were younger, but Auntie looked more tired.

"I'd recognize you anywhere, Fagel," said Auntie. "You look just like your father. You haven't changed a bit except now you are developing a woman's figure. On you it looks good."

30

I blushed.

"I'm sorry you had to stay so long on Ellis Island. Did they treat you nicely there?"

"Yes."

"Were you scared?" Itkeh jumped in.

"No."

"I don't believe you," she said loudly.

Then it all came back—what Itkeh had always been like, even when she was five—bossy.

"Now you remember your uncle," said Auntie, touching his shoulder.

"Hello, Uncle," I said to the pale, thin man who looked like Mother when she was sick. I shook his hand.

"And our girls," said Auntie.

The whole mob of them—maybe five or six— crowded around me.

"And the other relatives," said Auntie, gesturing to the other faces I didn't know in the room. "In the meantime, sit down, make yourself at home. Would you like a glass of tea? A piece of herring?"

"Tea, please," I said, sitting down.

I felt overwhelmed by all the people watching me.

Uncle began to cough again.

"Tomorrow," said Itkeh, "I will show you the real America, Cousin."

"So, tell me, how is your mother?" Auntie asked.

"Fine," I said. But was she? How could I know what was happening back home?

*C*HAPTER *6*

I went shopping in America with the cousins.

Itkeh doesn't let you forget she's the oldest. She's like a strict mother who keeps all the others in line. Itkeh issues her orders, then Libeh, who is next in age, makes sure the girls carry them out. Then there are Sadie and Bessie. Though they're the same age, it's hard to believe they are twins. Sadie is thin and her face looks pinched. She asks questions she shouldn't and says sour things. Bessie is round and has a sweet smile. She asks questions like, "Can I help you?" "How are you?" Zelda is eight years old, two years younger than the twins, and asthmatic. She stayed home today. No one seemed surprised that she didn't come. The littlest is Rosie. With her round face and features and well-proportioned body, she looks more like her father and our side of the family than do the other Lishofskys. They have that stocky, broad-shouldered build that shows they're hardworking people. Even at five, pretty Rosie likes to comb her hair in front of the mirror before leaving the house.

When she found out my name was Fagel, she made up a song: "Fagel-bird, Fagel-bird, when will you fly away? You flew to our house. Now, will you go away?"

I laughed when I heard it. Rosie's teasing made me feel right at home. I knew she was just being friendly, though Auntie wasn't pleased.

In Chelsea, you can hear Yiddish as well as English. Libeh explained that there were many Jewish families living near us. Polish people have houses near the factories on the water and the Irish have their own church, St. Rose's, in the center of town.

The cousins and I went to the Jewish marketplace on Arlington Street. It's only a few blocks from their house. Peddlers sell their wares out of pushcarts and stores display their best merchandise in glass windows. You can look in the window and see what they're doing too! The streets are straighter than in Slonim; you know you're in a city, not a country town. The signs are printed more clearly. Arlington

33

Street is cleaner than our marketplace but it's still filled with people strolling and watching and pushing and yelling, all at once. I love it!

Itkeh bargained with a man selling soap from a pushcart.

"Ten bars for a nickel," he said.

"A nickel?" asked Itkeh. "Some people have a lot of nerve."

"If you give me a nickel right now," he added, "I'll give you twelve."

"I'm not impressed," Sadie said.

"Thirteen and that's my final offer."

"I don't remember," said Libeh. "Is it the kind Mother uses?"

"Everybody needs soap," the man said. "Come see what I have."

"I want it," said Rosie. "Buy it, Itkeh."

"Shh," said Bessie.

Itkeh looked in the man's cart, and the other girls did too. She found only the grainy kind that rubs against the skin.

"We already have enough soap," she said. "Should we bother while we're showing our greenhorn cousin around?"

(Again that awful "green" word.)

"Fourteen is my final offer," said the man.

"All right," said Itkeh and took a nickel out of her cloth purse.

"You should have waited. He would have offered more," said Sadie.

34

"Hurrah," said Rosie, "I want a soap."

Then, even better, we went into a store where they sell ready-made clothes. All those cut-and-sewn skirts on one side, blouses on the other, and dresses in the center—in so many styles and colors! Who made them? How much work it must have taken!

"Come," said Itkeh, as she made her way toward the skirt rack.

"Can you actually buy things without ordering in advance?" I asked her.

"Of course, greenhorn," answered Itkeh, "just watch us do it."

I guessed she must know what she was doing. Itkeh always acted like she knew what she was doing and what everyone else was too. But I felt dishonest shopping without money or meaning to buy.

The girls poked through the racks. Itkeh pulled out one skirt and held it up next to herself.

"Do you like it?" she asked.

"It's too bright for you," said Libeh. "You're already big and tall enough without all that color."

"Thanks," said Itkeh.

"Don't ask if you don't want to know," Libeh answered.

Itkeh put the skirt back.

"Let's go," she said.

"Can I put a dress on?" asked Rosie.

"Not today," said Bessie softly.

"I want something," pleaded Rosie.

"Not today," repeated Itkeh more firmly.

We returned to the street.

"How did you know the skirt would fit?" I asked.

"All clothes are sized and you learn your number," said Itkeh.

"They let you try on things without buying?" I asked.

"Of course. How would they get a customer if they didn't?" Libeh explained.

"They need us. We don't need them," said Sadie.

I shrugged my shoulders; it seemed so strange that stores would waste their time dealing with people who weren't even going to be customers.

"Can you make a dress that good?" Bessie asked me.

"Yes, I think so."

"Then it's cheaper to make your own," she explained, "much."

We walked home as the sky was darkening. Street lamps came on but no one lit them. I asked the cousins how that was possible.

"Electricity," Libeh said, as if I was stupid.

I did feel stupid but I was also eager to learn about this new country.

CHAPTER 7

I remembered how I loved going to school in Slonim. Since I couldn't go to cheder with the boys, I used to study with Basha. I learned to copy writing and read a book, just like boys do, even if it is in Yiddish, not Hebrew.

Once Mother even praised me.

"I have a daughter who can read," she bragged to a customer.

Basha, my teacher, was sweet and pretty, and wore printed dresses with flowers on them. Basha was pleased when we read well.

Here in America, schools are very different.

When the morning came to go to school, I was scared but Bessie, Sadie, and Rosie were happy to be getting ready.

Sadie questioned if Bessie had her books.

"I don't know which books we need this year," said Bessie.

"Well, I'm bringing a clean, new notebook, two pencils, and last year's books," informed Sadie.

"That sounds good," Bessie answered in her care-free way.

"Well, I'm *always* prepared," said Sadie. "That's why I get better marks than you."

Rosie sang another made-up tune, "Fagel's going to school. Fagel's going to school."

I sang "Raizele" to myself. If my own mother couldn't be with me, at least my own song could.

"Here we are," said Auntie, standing in front of a serious-looking building.

I didn't like that place with the American flag flying on the roof. It was too strict. It could have been Ellis Island. What kind of teachers could be in a place like that?

"I hope you have a very good first day at our Cary School," wished Bessie.

"Good luck," said Sadie.

Rosie threw her arms around me.

"Bye, Fagel," they all said, leaving Auntie and me in the lobby, where more little girls talking to each other passed by.

Inside the main office, Auntie waited before a desk where many grown-up people were speaking to each other in English.

I tugged at Auntie's skirt.

"What is it?" she asked in our Yiddish.

"Can I speak to you?"

I left that office and waited in the hall, where she followed me. Not understanding why, I just kept walking until I was outside of that building. Auntie followed me again.

"What is it, Fagel? Why are we out here?"

"I don't want to go to that school."

"So," said Auntie, "we'll go home."

"But will they arrest me?"

"Don't be silly."

"What if they find out I'm not in school?"

"Who finds out?"

"The government, the neighbors, the school."

"Ah, this is Chelsea, in America. No one reports on you."

"But I'm supposed to go to school."

"Yes, Fagel," said Auntie, "and you will, later. For now, you won't. You can stay home and keep me company—not bad at all. So let's go."

All the way back, I felt littler and littler, like a dumb greenhorn. But to tell the truth, a few days later, I wasn't sorry. Sitting around with the cousins, I learn English words. I already know: *hello*, *good-bye*, *lunch*, *paycheck*, *girl*, *boy*. I heard more words on Arlington Street and in synagogue. When I start working, I'll learn more.

If Auntie says I don't have to go to school now, I'm not going. I don't want to be the class idiot. After all, I'm a nice person but I'm not brilliant like Pinchas.

CHAPTER 8

Auntie found me a job. I am sewing children's clothes for a lady from Ayuda Achim Synagogue, Mrs. Goodman. Her husband owns a bar-restaurant which does quite well. I think she hired me because she feels sorry for Auntie with all her children to feed and now a new one. Certainly, Mrs. Goodman could afford to buy ready-mades for her family, but I don't care. I'm very glad to be working and making money.

So when the other girls go off to jobs or school, I stay home with Auntie and make the clothes. Auntie tells me her troubles and asks about Mother.

Yesterday she said, "Tell me the truth. How did your mother look the last time you saw her? How was she feeling?"

"She looked fine," I said, recalling the day we went to the woods together.

"It was so hard for her after your father, may he rest in peace, died. So many little children to care for," Auntie sighed.

I said nothing. What could I say to that?

"Well, she's a sturdy woman and she'll do all right," Auntie sighed again. "God knows it's lucky there are strong women around. What would the world do without us?"

I nodded.

"You know, Fagel," Auntie began again, "your mother was such a beautiful girl. We used to have good times together when we were young. We'd go off in the woods and gather berries. We'd laugh. Oh, how we'd laugh. And she was such a good dancer. Did you know that? She loved to dance and sing. You're only a girl for a little while, Fagel. You have to appreciate it while you can. All too soon, you get married and have responsibilities, and children, and worries. Listen, I know, it's far from easy being a mother.

"God forbid, I'm not complaining but if it weren't for me, this family would fall apart. Your uncle, Moishe, is a good man, a religious one. He works hard even though he's not well, but he couldn't keep this family together for a minute without me."

Auntie talks like this all the time. I'm happy to hear stories of Mother when she was young. But I already have my own sad memories and fears; I don't want to hear more. I want to hear music.

Well, yesterday I had other company besides Auntie. My favorite, Rosie, took the day off from school. She just didn't want to go.

She spent a good part of the day standing in front of the mirror, combing her hair, putting a ribbon in, taking it out, turning to one side, then the other, to see which way she looked best. Then she came into the kitchen where I was alone (Auntie had gone to the store) and asked which style suited her better.

"I like the blue ribbon best," I told her honestly.

"Fagel, Fagel, Fagel," she began a made-up song. "Are you a bird? Will you fly back to the old country?"

I laughed. Sometimes I wish I were a bird who could fly back and forth between the old and new worlds.

"No, Rosie, I'm here to take care of you."

"Tell me about the old country, Fagel."

"Which story?"

"Tell me how you learned to sew."

"Well, every day I got up early to go to Mr. Antowicki's house in town. In his parlor, he taught ten apprentices. We learned to make an entire dress."

"How much did he pay you, Fagel?"

"Nothing, Rosie. My mother paid him to teach me a trade."

"Your mother gave him money?"

"Yes."

"Fagel," said Rosie, walking around the kitchen, "guess what I want to do?"

"I don't know. Tell me."

"You guess."

"Learn a trade?"

"No. Get married now."

"But, Rosie, you're only five years old."

"I know, but if I'm married, I'd only have to share my bedroom with one other person."

"And have a lot of responsibilities, like making dinner for your husband every night?"

"I could always go to the store and buy a herring."

I laughed. It was fun to have Rosie home and be able to play big sister again.

Usually, I can hardly wait until after three o'clock when the door opens and Sadie, Bessie, Zelda, and Rosie tumble in from school. Then, several hours later, come Itkeh and Libeh, followed by their father, and the evening meal. After dinner, the girls sit around talking. This is the happiest part of my day. They sing American songs too, which I try to memorize. Here's a popular one I did learn:

"Take me out to the ballgame,
Take me out with the crowd.
Buy me some peanuts and crackerjack,

I don't care if I never come back.
Let me root, root, root for the home
   team...
If they don't win, it's a shame.
For it's one, two, three strikes, you're out
At the old ballgame."

Bessie translated the words into Yiddish. They're funny, not full of meaning like Hatzkel's workers' songs or of romance like my "Raizele." Imagine singing about a game where a grown man uses a wooden stick to hit a ball! The music is funnier still. The melody is not like our rich, full ones. Our simple Jewish or Russian songs make you laugh or cry. Do people keep alive the warmth of their Jewish hearts here in America? I don't know.

_C_HAPTER _9_

The other day a man taps at the door. Auntie opens it, recognizes him, and invites him in. He is a peddler carrying a knapsack which weighs him down. He sells dresses Auntie can't afford. Even knowing this, he still comes.

"Good morning, housewife," he began, "I have a lovely dress for you."

"Let's see," said Auntie.

He took out a long, light blue dress and held it up for her to see.

"Not bad," said Auntie.

"Beautiful," said the peddler.

"How much?" asked Auntie.

"Only three dollars," said the peddler.

"Too much," said Auntie.

"Listen," he said, "you pay me a dollar fifty now, one dollar next week, and fifty cents the week after, and it's yours to wear right now."

"Still too much," said Auntie. "Who do you think I am? A millionaire?"

"Two is the lowest I can go," the peddler said. "I have a family to feed too."

"Well," considered Auntie, "no, I can't."

"All right," he said, "what about the girl?"

"Oh, my niece?" Auntie said. "She just got off the boat. She can't afford your prices."

Thanks a lot, I thought. "Just got off the boat . . . greenhorn . . ." Why do the Lishofskys have to keep bringing this up? I don't call them names!

"So, she still has to wear clothes," he said.

"Yes," agreed Auntie, "thank God she's handy with a needle herself. Here, look at her work."

She showed him the shirt I was making (it's like the sailor shirts I made for Herschel, Zelig, and Pinchas).

"Very nice," said the peddler. "I must be on my way. Stay healthy, ladies."

Now, why did he spend so much time when he knew she wouldn't buy? Is it like the store I went into with the cousins, where they wander around without buying? I don't understand. If you want a dress, you order one. If you don't, why do the salesmen spend time with you?

"Aii, Fagel," Auntie is talking again. "I worry so much about Moishe. It's his lungs, you know. He's weak."

I certainly know about weak lungs. My father died from pneumonia.

"It's not good. I think he'd be fired from his job by now if he didn't work for a relative. I know he works hard but he's slower than the other workers. And his cough, it gets worse. You never know.

"We barely have enough as it is. We just get by with the little Itkeh and Libeh give. What if he really got sick and couldn't work? What would we do then? Beg? Starve? With six children and a seventh on the way?"

I didn't answer her because I didn't know what to say. I'm worried about money too. With the little I have, I want to save as much as possible in order to send home the first ticket. Should I give money to Auntie and Uncle?

I almost quit my job yesterday. I was so insulted, I really wanted to quit.

When I brought the clothes to Mrs. Goodman's, she smiled as sweetly as she always does. She was wearing a taffeta-striped dress with her dark hair piled up on her head and real jewels, as if she was going to have tea in a Boston hotel.

Then she asked me to sit down. I did—in one of those plush velvet chairs that you just sink into. She left the room and I looked around. There were pictures in dark wood frames all over the walls, scenes of the nearby ocean and others of forests and mountains—all very tasteful and restful. Then there were the matching chairs and the couch in dark rose velvet, many little tables covered with long cloths fringed on the bottom. Photographs of her family in silver frames clustered next to objects made of marble and wood, some of animals, some of people. And best of all, my eyes feasted on the upright piano in the corner. Oh, would I love to learn how to play it!

Mrs. Goodman returned, carrying a silver tray with a silver teapot, two china cups and saucers, and a platter of cookies. She set the tray on the largest table and poured me a cup of steaming hot tea.

As she sat, she tugged at the top of her dress, but it was no use—the expensive material couldn't expand enough to cover her wide body.

"Have a cookie, please," she said, passing the platter.

"Thank you," I said, taking a dark chocolate one.

"Well, Fagel," she said, "I'm very happy with your sewing for my boys."

"Thank you," I repeated.

"And I'm very pleased to know as nice a girl as you."

"Thank you."

"It must be very crowded living with your cousins," she added quickly.

"We manage."

"You're lucky they took you in."

"Yes, I am."

"I don't mean to be forward," Mrs. Goodman said, leaning toward me as she spoke, "but I couldn't help noticing since we only have four people in our big home . . ."

I waited for her to continue.

"Actually, I've been thinking about this for a while. I spoke to Mr. Goodman last night and said wouldn't it be nice if we could ask a young girl to live here and help us. He agreed.

"You could do other things than sew, Fagel. You could help watch my boys and work in the kitchen too. I'd give you double the amount you make now, in addition to free room and board."

My ears began to burn. I couldn't believe what I was hearing.

When I finally felt words come out of my mouth, I answered.

"No, I couldn't. I have to go. Thank you for the tea and cookies. I'll see you next week."

"All right, Fagel, but please think over my offer."

As I walked back to the Lishofskys, I stamped my feet hard on the sidewalk. I felt so angry and insulted. Who did she think I was? Did she think I was only a servant? Didn't she realize that I had trained to be a dressmaker? Our mother worked hard to teach her children trades so they wouldn't have to live in other people's houses. What would Mother think if she knew I moved out of the Lishofskys and went to live like an ignorant serving girl in a stranger's house! Father would roll over in his grave.

If Hatzkel were here, he would shout about the workers and the rich. Maybe right now I would agree with him. Zelig thinks that the streets of America are paved with gold. That's a lie. The New World is just like the old. Rich people think they're better than poor people and that they can buy us. Well, I'm not for sale. I will not dishonor my family. I will not pretend that I come from nowhere or have no profession or people I belong to.

CHAPTER 10

Last night Itkeh, Libeh, and I went dancing! We took the streetcar into Boston. We paid at the door of a large room with a good wooden floor. An orchestra was playing. Many couples were dancing and other young men and women were wandering around with cups in their hands. Off to one side, a man was demonstrating dance steps while people followed him.

I loved it immediately.

I even recognized many of the tunes, some Russian, some Jewish, that we danced to in Europe. I hummed along until Libeh asked me to dance. As we moved, she pointed out people she recognized. A boy who worked with Uncle had brought his brother. How handsome that brother, called Shlomo, was! You should have seen his eyes; they were dark as coal. The way he stared, you just had to look away or those eyes would eat you up. Libeh said that this Shlomo didn't work but always dressed well. Weeks ago she had talked to him and he said that the economy of the United States stinks.

"It's only right to take from the rich who have too much, to give to the poor who need it," he told Libeh.

Libeh said that was crazy; he was a thief, pure and simple.

I wasn't so sure. It sounded right to me, especially when I thought of Hatzkel and his revolutionary friends who are proud to be on the side of the people.

"Revolutionary, my eye," Libeh answered when I told her my thought. "Shlomo just doesn't like to work like honest people do."

It was hard not to look at him. His clothes fitted better than any other boy there and those eyes . . . I tried not to let him see me gazing at him. I didn't want to give him the wrong impression.

When Libeh and I stopped dancing, we went to get a drink. I turned to watch the dance floor and sing along again. Then I heard a masculine voice say I sang well. I turned around to see a boy standing next to me. He looked a few years older and stood a bit taller than me. Something about him reminded me of our father, serious but kind.

"Thank you," I answered him softly.

"You're welcome," he said. "Would you care to dance?"

"Well, yes," I agreed.

At first, I felt funny and had trouble following him. I wondered what Daddy would think of my going to a hired hall and dancing with a stranger. It's different from dancing with a new boy at a wedding where everyone's been invited. I hoped Daddy would understand that I had to have fun sometimes.

After a few songs, I relaxed. Soon the sounds of the music filled my body as well as my ears and dancing became fun.

When we stopped, we sat down on some chairs at the side of the hall.

"Where do you come from?"

"Slonim."

"Oh, you're a newcomer?"

"Yes." (Newcomer is a nicer word than greenhorn.)

"No wonder I haven't seen you before. Where do you live?"

"In Chelsea."

"Do you rent a bed?"

"Oh, no, I stay with my cousins."

"Oh, I didn't mean to pry. A lot of people don't live with their families."

"Oh, what do they do?"

"They rent a bed, live where they work, do whatever they can to survive."

"Do you live with your family?"

"Yes. I live with my brother, sisters, father and mother. What's your name. Mine's Herschel."

"That's my brother's name. I'm Fagel."

"Is your brother here tonight?"

"Oh, no, he's still in Russia."

"Did you come to America alone?"

"Yes and no. My uncle brought me but my brothers and sisters and mother are still in Russia."

"You must be very courageous to come without them."

"You think so?"

"Yes, I think so. Even though I came with my family, I felt strange for a long time. There's so much to learn and unlearn so quickly."

"Yes, it's true."

I felt good talking to him.

Itkeh walked by and motioned with her hand that she wanted to leave.

"Excuse me, I have to go now," I told this Herschel.

"I enjoyed talking to you. I hope to see you again."

"Same here, likewise."

"I come every Saturday."

"So do my cousins."

"See you next week."

"Yes, see you next week."

Then I ran to find Itkeh who hurried me off to the room where we had put our coats.

"So you got a live one, eh, Fagel?" said Itkeh.

I blushed.

"Don't go believing everything he says, just because he looks good."

She tried to rush Libeh and me out the door, but I delayed long enough to see who won the dancing contest, and their prizes. The girl got a Chinese red-lacquered fan and the boy won a leather wallet.

Then the three of us walked all the way back to Chelsea, singing. The streetcar had stopped running at midnight and walking was the only way to get home.

"Did you see what Fagel picked up?" Itkeh said after we had finished singing.

"Not bad," said Libeh.

"Not good," said Itkeh. "A real nobody."

I pretended not to hear. I didn't want their words to ruin my fun. Herschel was someone who understood me. I was sure of that.

CHAPTER *11*

Yesterday was terrible.

Uncle's horse died. He caught his hoof between the cobblestones and howled in pain. They had to shoot him to end his misery. So Uncle and Auntie didn't go to synagogue today. All the girls went, as usual, but I had to finish a shirt. While I worked in the kitchen, I heard shouts coming from Auntie and Uncle's bedroom.

"I don't know," Auntie repeated. "I don't know. You have to do *something*."

"What should I do?" Uncle answered quietly, sounding resigned.

"You can't stay home. You have to have a job. We have to feed the children."

"Should I ask for a job in the junkyard and sell the cart?"

"You can't work there. It's too much dust for your lungs."

"But what can I do with just the cart?"

"Nothing. That's what you can do."

When I heard that Uncle's horse was shot, I thought about another horse and cart and about the funeral that Nahamkah, Blume, and I didn't attend. Only the boys got to go because they say prayers for the dead. But I've never forgotten the sounds of that day in Slonim; the cobblestones seemed to creak as the cart carried our father to the cemetery. Even inside the house, I could follow the sounds of Daddy being taken away from us.

The loud voices began again.

"You have to get another horse," Auntie screamed. "That's all there is to it."

"Who will give me two hundred and fifty dollars?"

"Someone. Someone must."

"But who?"

"Ahhh," screeched Auntie, a wail so loud it pierced my ears. "Ahhh, his children are going to starve and he doesn't want he should ask a relative."

She ran from the back of the house to the kitchen where I sat.

"Fagel, go find the girls at the synagogue."

"Yes, Auntie."

She hurried to the back of the house.

I heard Uncle say, "And now we have another one to feed."

"Yes," said Auntie, "but she's *your* niece, not mine."

I ran out of the house as quickly as I could. I had heard too much already. I didn't want to go to the synagogue. I didn't want to see any more Lishofskys. That's why I went toward Broadway, where the Goodman bar-restaurant was, humming "Raizele," wishing someone was calling me.

I wasn't going to see Mrs. Goodman, but on Broadway, I wouldn't see anyone else who would recognize me. As I neared Chelsea Square, on Broadway, I saw a long line, coming from a theater. I couldn't read the marquee or ask someone in English what was playing. But, so what, I thought to myself, it had to be theater or music and that had to be good, so I joined the line.

When it began to move, I saw people hand over a dime to get inside. I did too. Sitting in my seat, I could hardly wait for the performance to begin.

But then I thought of Daddy and wondered what he would say. What if he would be angry that I chose music over synagogue? I didn't care.

This is the New World, filled with new ways that I have to try out.

First, two men in baggy suits came out and talked fast to each other. The audience laughed. I wished I could have understood what they were saying.

Still, guessing from the way they moved, slapping their legs, and shaking hands, I figured they were comedians. I even laughed when one slipped on a banana peel.

Next came three men dressed in striped shirts and suspenders, each playing an instrument like a balalaika but round. I loved how they plucked the strings and sang.

Afterward, a juggler twirled three balls at once. Then he used wooden sticks and things that seemed on fire. I wonder if they really were or how he got them to look like that.

Then came the magician. He pulled a rabbit out of a big black hat, and an egg that wasn't in his hand appeared out of nowhere. So did some white handkerchiefs.

The last was the best: Photographs in black and white moved across the stage. It was utterly amazing. These picture people were larger than life, and sometimes only their faces showed, so big you couldn't believe it. After a scene ended, written words appeared on the screen. A man and woman sang along with a piano the whole time.

Even without reading, I could understand the story. They were lovers; he was from a rich family and she was poor. They fell in love when he stayed at the hotel where she was the chambermaid. His family was against her. Rather than start a family fight, she ran away. When he couldn't find her, he agreed to marry the girl his family had chosen for him, but he wasn't happy. Finally he decided to search for his true love, only to find her on her death bed.

When the lights came back on, it seemed that I had returned from a far place, a place that made me very happy even if I felt sorry for the girl.

As I made my way back to Auntie's, I hummed the tune I'd heard at the deliciously sad movie.

Quietly, I hurried into the house and the bedroom. I hoped no one would hear me. Much to my surprise, Libeh, Itkeh, Bessie, Sadie, Zelda, and Rosie were all assembled in the bedroom.

"So there you are," said Libeh.

"Where have you been, cousin Fagel?" asked Itkeh. "We were worried about you. You're lucky we waited here for you without telling our parents."

"I . . . I . . . I went to the theater," I stammered.

"*What?*" barked Itkeh.

I began to cry.

"Leave her alone," said Bessie.

"Why didn't you tell us?" demanded Sadie.

"You went to the theater instead of synagogue?" said Libeh.

"You didn't tell us," repeated Itkeh.

I couldn't stop crying. Bessie put her arms around me.

"Let her be," she said to her sisters. To me, she added, "Don't worry."

I looked up. Just like her arms had warmed my body, her face warmed my heart.

"Fagel," Bessie continued, "there is nothing to worry about. Mother and Father have gone to the Hebrew Loan Society. They'll have a new horse tomorrow and they'll get the money without interest. It's all very lucky.

"Better yet, next week, when there's no work and after Sabbath, we'll take you someplace special."

CHAPTER 12

Bessie was as good as her word. We seven all got up early and packed a lunch to take with us.

Out into the clear dawn we went. Before leaving the building, we checked the mailbox, just in case there was something not picked up yesterday. There was a letter for me! I looked at the return address and was pleased to see it was from Mother. I decided to save the letter until I would have time to read and reread every precious word, so I put it in my pocket. We rushed to make the trolley but I didn't know where we were going. Bessie had hinted that we were leaving Chelsea. I stared out the window, happy to be moving along to someplace new.

"We'll be at Revere Beach soon," said Libeh.

"The beach?" I asked.

"Yes," smiled Bessie, "that's where we're going."

"Hurrah," I shouted.

The trolley stopped and out we marched, follow-the-leader style. We strolled down a broad roadway.

Pointing to a large brick building, Itkeh said, "That's where we rent and change into bathing suits."

"Bathing suits?" I asked. "What're they?"

"What you wear to swim in," Itkeh answered impatiently. "We don't wear our underwear *here*."

"But I used to go in the water in Slonim."

"Sure, hidden in some shack. Here you have everything—sand, ocean, food stands, restaurants, hotels, rides, an amusement park, dance halls . . . It's our own Coney Island."

"Can we go on a ride?" I asked as we made our way toward the sand.

"Not today, Cousin," she answered. "The season closed after Labor Day, but next summer you can get scared on Shooting-the-Chutes."

"The best shows are at Wonderland Amusement Park," said Sadie. "They set fire to a building and then a whole hook and ladder company rushes in to put it out."

"Last summer's carnival, they made a volcano right on the beach," laughed Bessie.

"What?" I asked.

"They built this huge cone out of papier-mâché and smoke came roaring out of the top, just like a real volcano."

"And what about the diving horses and the floats and costumes and parades and fireworks?" added Sadie.

"And the band concerts," said Libeh.

"Taffy," said Rosie, "I want taffy."

"Later," said Itkeh. "Before we go home, we'll stop by the fish stand and buy our saltwater taffy."

We had finally arrived at the Atlantic Ocean, the same one I had traveled on to get here. How beautiful it was. It went on forever, while the waves came rushing to the shore, sounding their loud call.

On this pleasant fall day there weren't many people. Itkeh picked a spot to spread out the blanket. Then all the girls took off their shoes and put them on the edge so it wouldn't blow away.

Itkeh, Libeh, and I sat down. Sadie and Bessie ran to the water.

"Don't go in," Itkeh screamed.

"We're just going to put our toes in," Sadie yelled back.

"No farther, or you'll come back here."

Rosie and Zelda stayed on the sand. They picked it up and let it fall through their open fingers. Then they got down to work. Zelda borrowed a cup from the wicker basket to fill with ocean water and make the sand like clay, easy to build with.

I loved watching them play. I don't remember such carefree moments in Slonim. We were always working—learning a trade, doing chores. I never had dolls or other playthings. Just to be able to look at the water on one side and the food stands and rides on the other made me happy.

When Zelda returned with ocean water, Rosie began to construct a castle.

"Here, Fagel," Rosie directed, "pour some water into the river. Then the people who live in the castle can have fish to catch for dinner. We have to have enough water for the fish to live in."

As I was pouring from the cup, I remembered the letter I had put in my pocket that morning.

"Rosie," I said, "I have to do something first. I'll be back."

"Don't be long, Fagel. The fish will get thirsty."

"I won't," I promised.

Then I moved to a corner of the blanket, far from Itkeh and Libeh, and pulled out the letter. In silence I read.

October 4, 1907

My Dearest Fagel,

I hope you and the whole Lishofsky family are well. Here in Slonim, we are well too.

I have many serious things to say to you,

*Fagel, little bird, so I hope you will listen well.
I wish you were here right now so I could say
them in person. It is so much harder to put
them down in a letter, like you do so well,
but I will try.*

*I get a very different picture of America
from your letters than from Auntie's. I didn't
realize that Uncle was still coughing. I didn't
know that they were expecting their seventh
child. You are not to show this letter to them,
ever. No one told me that they are struggling
so much.*

*The used clothes I trade bring in some
money. Add that to the rent from the house
your father built and the fruits I sell when
they're ripe. So, you see, we're not doing badly
anymore.*

*If you want to come home, I can send you
money as I promised. Do you want to, Fagel,
dear?*

*You are not to send us any money. If you
decide to stay in America, you must continue
to give yours to Auntie and Uncle. With their
problems, they need it. They have taken you
in and treated you like their own. You are.
You belong to them as well as to us.*

*I am your mother and miss you all the time,
but I do not know when I will see you. Now
that things are going better, it seems easier
for us to stay put. If I send anyone, it will be*

Blume. But I will not send her to America. I can't give the Lishofskys anymore than they already have. I'm considering Argentina. The family there has been asking me to send someone, so we'll see.

Now, little one, you must continue to be brave and think of happy things and not complain. A lot of people have helped you along so far. So will others. Remember that.

We miss you all the time. Little Herschel keeps asking where you went.

Please write and let me know your decision. We are sending you all our love.

From the bottom of my heart,

Your Mamenyu,
Shaneh Gittel

_C_HAPTER _13_

I went to the waves.

Only they could touch my aching heart.

Forward they rolled, then back. If only I could see and hear the waves, then all the other voices in my head would be drowned out.

Forward went the waves, then back.

I couldn't forget Mother's letter. I felt as if I didn't belong anywhere.

Should I go back? To the trees? But how could I? What would I be going back to? Hatzkel lives in Bialystok, at least for now, and who knows where he'll be next. Blume could be in Argentina next month. And where will Pinchas and Zelig go? The place I want to go back to is with our family happy and whole, when Daddy was with us, and that is gone forever.

As the waves rolled, they seemed to be talking to me.

Forward you go, you can't go back, they seemed to be saying.

There is no back to go back to. I must take care of myself and others the way Daddy once took care of us.

The waves are right. Forward you go. You can't go back.

Forward, forward, forward.

And my family is coming with me. I will not give up on them. First, my flowering cherry, Blume, will come here, not to Argentina. Next, Hatzkel, my strong spruce, will leave Bialystok. Then my upright tamarack, Pinchas, and my curving pine, Zelig, will come. And of course, our delicate dogwood, Nahamkah, our mulberry sapling, Herschel, and our sheltering linden, Mamenyu, will join us.

I will bring them all here.

Yes, I will!

CHAPTER *14*

The next morning, I got up and folded the clothes I had sewn for Mrs. Goodman, said good-bye to Auntie, and left the house.

On the five blocks over to Mrs. Goodman's I walked very tall. Nothing could stop me now.

I knocked at her door and she smiled when she let me in.

"It's good to see you, Fagel," she said. "Please sit down."

I put the pile of clothing on a chair.

"Mrs. Goodman," I said, "I've reconsidered my decision."

"Does that mean you will be coming to live with us?" she said.

I nodded my head, yes.

"Oh, how wonderful," said Mrs. Goodman. "I know Mr. Goodman and Stewart and Cabot will be so glad. When I mentioned that you might be coming to live with us before, they were very pleased."

"Thank you," I said.

"Well," she said, "maybe I should show you where you will sleep."

I followed her down the hall past the dining room. She opened the second door. Inside was a bed with a flowered cover, a tall, dark wood dresser, a wooden desk with its own chair, an easy chair, and a rug on the floor.

"This will be your room," she said.

I could hardly believe it. I just stood and stared. This was hardly treating me like a servant. I've never had my own bed, let alone my own room, and it was just as beautifully decorated as the rest of the house.

Mrs. Goodman spoke again.

"Is this acceptable to you?"

"Oh, yes," I said, "it's fine, just fine, thank you."

"Good," she said, "but you haven't brought your things."

Things, I thought—all I owned could fit into one drawer.

"No," I answered, "I have to go back to my aunt's to pack."

"Fine," she said. "Then shall I expect you for lunch or dinner?"

"Dinner," I said.

We walked back to the front of the house.

"There are the clothes I made for the boys," I said, pointing to the stack on the chair.

"So I see," she said. "We'll talk about your other duties later, probably tomorrow."

"Yes," I agreed.

"And you'll meet Stewart and Cabot for the first time," she sighed.

"Yes."

"They're six and seven. You know, I named them after the people in the Society Pages I read in the newspaper," she smiled.

"Oh," I said. "Well, good-bye for now."

"Good-bye, Fagel."

For the first block as I walked back to the Lishofskys', I practically sailed. My own room! I felt like a princess. By the third block, I steeled myself to face Auntie. What would she say?

"Auntie," I said, as soon as I entered the door, "I am going to be living with the Goodmans to earn more money."

"What?" she said. "What did I hear you say?"

Rosie came into the kitchen from the bedroom.

"You didn't go to school today?" I asked.

Rosie smiled and shook her head.

Pale Zelda, rubbing the sleep from her eyes, joined us.

73

"Forget her and Zelda too," said Auntie. "Now what did you say, Fagel?"

I repeated it.

"You are going to leave the house of relatives who sent for you, who sheltered you, who are the only family you have here, to live with strangers? Is that what I heard you say?"

"Auntie, it's not like that."

"Oh no, it's a shame on me and your uncle and your cousins. Everyone will point at us. We made our greenhorn cousin live with strangers! Are we so cruel that we throw out our own?"

"Auntie, please listen. I know what you're thinking, but it doesn't have to be like that. Really."

"Then how is it?"

"My mother doesn't have to know if you don't tell her."

"You're asking me to lie?"

"The rabbi says it's not wrong to break a rule if you're saving someone's life."

"And whose life are we saving? Tell me."

"Maybe Blume, maybe Nahamkah, or my mother or Herschel or Zelig or Hatzkel."

"How?"

"If I can get them out of Europe sooner rather than later, maybe, you can never tell, I might be saving their lives."

"How?"

"Mrs. Goodman is going to pay me double what she pays now. Then I get free room and board.

Maybe I can do a little extra sewing on the side. That way I can save more and send for them sooner."

"So," said Auntie, sitting down.

"And there's another thing . . . it's not that I don't appreciate all you've done for me. You take very good care of me. You didn't have to ask for another child, especially when you have so many of your own."

Auntie breathed a sigh.

I went on, "And soon you'll have another."

"But we wouldn't throw you out on the street like poor, ignorant people do."

"Of course not, Auntie."

"Fagel's flying away," sang Rosie.

"Hush," said her mother.

"It's not as if I'm going to strangers. You've known the Goodmans for years. You introduced me. They belong to your synagogue. It's not a shame, it's an honor. One of your children has been chosen to help out a friend."

"Well," said Auntie, "let me think about it."

I walked back to the bedroom and began to pack my clothes. Rosie followed.

"Fagel . . . ," she said.

I hugged her tight.

"Are you really leaving us, flying away?"

"Oh no, Rosie. I don't ever want to leave you. I'm only going five blocks away to get a better job. I can see you all the time."

"That's good," said Rosie.

When all my things were in the trunk, I pulled it back into the kitchen I had first entered when I came to America. Auntie was boiling clothes clean on the stove. She looked around.

"I've been thinking, little Fagel," she said, "this may not be a bad idea. You come here every Friday night for Sabbath dinner and the rest of the week, it will be like you're working someplace else."

"Yes, Auntie."

"And we'll all be together on Saturdays."

"Yes."

"And I can tell Uncle what a good girl you are, to work so hard for your family. Everyone can understand that."

"And Auntie . . ."

"Yes, Fagel?"

"You won't tell my mother?"

"What's to tell? There's nothing to say. If you want to tell her you switched jobs, you can. We're still your family and watching out for you. Right?"

"Yes, Auntie."

"So, it's understood?"

"Yes, Auntie," I said, as I put an arm around Rosie.

CHAPTER 15

This afternoon I found out why Mrs. Goodman hired me.

After unpacking my trunk, I joined her in the living room. As we were talking, the door opened. In burst two running boys. The smaller one threw his books on the floor and ran to the back of the house, followed by the plain, tall one who looks like his mother. They didn't even stop to say hello. From the bedroom, we could hear yelling.

"Did you take my books again?" shouted Stewart.

"Not me," answered Cabot.

"Yes, you did," said Stewart, "and you're going to pay for it too."

"Excuse me," said Mrs. Goodman, going to the back of the house.

I just sat there.... What else could I do? I had only met the boys once before, in passing, so I had no idea what to expect. I knew their clothing sizes perfectly, but not their personalities....

"Now, boys, calm down," Mrs. Goodman's voice carried.

"He's teasing me again," yelled Stewart.

"Ha, ha, ha," said Cabot.

"Now, boys, I want you to meet someone who came especially to see you," said Mrs. Goodman.

"I don't want to," said Cabot.

"Stop hitting," said Mrs. Goodman.

"He started it," said Stewart.

"Ha, ha, ha," said Cabot.

"Please stop hitting," said Mrs. Goodman.

Loud noises filled the air.

Mrs. Goodman came back to the living room.

"If you want to meet the boys, you'd better come to their bedroom," she said.

I followed her.

Cabot and Stewart were hitting each other with pillows.

"Boys," said Mrs. Goodman, "here's the person I want you to meet."

Just when Stewart turned to look at me, Cabot hit him with the pillow.

"Take that," said Cabot.

"I have three younger brothers," I told them.

The pillows continued to fly.

"Please, boys, be polite," begged Mrs. Goodman.

The fight continued.

It ended only when the boys had exhausted themselves and let the pillows drop to the floor.

"Cabot and Stewart, this is Fagel, the nice girl I was telling you about," said Mrs. Goodman.

This time both boys looked at me.

"Hello, Stewart. Hello, Cabot. It's nice to meet you," I said, though I certainly wondered if that were true.

"Hello," said Stewart. "Mother told us you would be coming."

"Hello," said Cabot.

"Are you going to stay here?" Stewart asked.

"Yes," I said.

"Why?" asked Cabot.

"Now, Cabot," said Mrs. Goodman, "I told you that Fagel would be helping us out."

"But why?" Cabot asked again.

"It's not easy to run a house alone," said Mrs. Goodman.

Cabot shrugged his shoulders.

Stewart took the marbles off his desk and began to throw them until they rebounded off the opposite wall.

Cabot began to bounce on the bed. The springs started to squeak and he bounced higher.

Mrs. Goodman grabbed my arm and pulled me toward the kitchen. She opened a cabinet above the sink and took out a bottle of pills. She took two with water.

"Those boys always give me a headache," she said.

I nodded and thought to myself, I can see why.

"Are you hungry?" she asked.

"Yes."

"Well, let's get the boys and go," she said.

She returned to the boys' bedroom.

"Cabot and Stewart," she yelled, "we're going to the restaurant."

"Hurrah," said Cabot.

The four of us walked down the stairs and entered the bottom floor of the building. Inside it was dark. A long bar with stools lined one side. Behind it was a long mirror and more bottles than I can ever remember seeing. A bald man wearing a bow tie, who stood behind the bar, was pouring a drink for a customer. The barman looked up when we entered.

"Hello, Mrs. Goodman," he said.

"Hello, Archie," she answered. "Is Mr. Goodman here?"

"He's back in the restaurant," Archie said, "and Cabot and Stewart, how are you?"

They ignored him.

Passing many small tables, we walked to the next room. There the tables were not only bigger, they were covered with red-and-white-checked tablecloths. The lights were brighter too. In the back, resting a large arm on the fireplace mantel, was a robust man, talking loudly.

When Cabot saw him, he yelled, "Daddy!" and ran to him.

"Cabot," said the big man with a barrel chest, who clearly was Mr. Goodman. He looked just like Cabot, grown up. "Go sit with your mother at table six. I'll join you in a minute."

"All right, Daddy," said Cabot.

We went to sit at a table in the corner. Both Cabot and Stewart sat quietly, hands folded on the table, feet still.

I could hardly believe that these two boys, who, only minutes before, had run wild, could act so peaceably now.

Soon the portly man arrived at our table, pulled up a large wooden chair between Mrs. Goodman and Stewart, and sat down.

"So," he addressed me, "you must be Fagel. I'm Mr. Goodman. Glad to meet you."

He put out his hand for me to shake.

Then he addressed Cabot and Stewart.

"So, how was school today?"

"Fine," they said in unison.

"And how was after-school today?"

The boys directed their eyes to the floor.

"I'm counting on you to behave," said their father. "Now, let's eat."

"Shall I get you a menu, Fagel? We have a beef stew that's very fresh, very good."

"I'll have the beef," I said.

I smiled. It was fun to be ordering dinner in a nice restaurant. There were definitely some advantages to this job.

"Well, Fagel," said Mr. Goodman, returning to the table, "I can handle the food... can you handle these young ones?"

"I think so," I said.

Cabot and Stewart looked at me.

And I am going to handle it. It's more money than I could get anyplace else. I'm used to taking care of children. I don't want to lose this job, so I'll find some way to deal with these rascals.

CHAPTER 16

I already have five dollars saved and I think it's going to be much easier to get the money together than I would have guessed. I no longer have to give half my earnings to Auntie and Uncle because I don't live there. When I go to visit on Friday nights, I bring two large challah breads, which Mr. Goodman gets at a discount through the restaurant.

Last Friday, when I went for dinner, I brought Rosie some ribbons I had picked up in a nearby store. I helped her tie them in her hair before we all sat down to eat.

When Auntie lit the candles, I actually felt thankful. Since I didn't live there full-time, I was glad to see everyone. I even laughed when Itkeh asked, "So, how are the boys?"

"Not bad," I answered.

"That's something," she answered. "Everyone says they can't be controlled."

"That's right," said Sadie, "you should see them at synagogue. Out the door they run, even on the Sabbath. They're always teasing other children."

"Well," said Bessie, "who wants more kugel? It's delicious."

Itkeh said, "Tomorrow we're going dancing. Too bad you can't go with us."

"Why not?" I asked. "I can go with you."

"Now, Fagel," said Auntie, returning with more chicken and sitting herself down slowly, "be careful. You have a good job and you don't want to lose it."

"What do you mean?" I asked.

"Maybe Mrs. Goodman doesn't want you to leave the house every night. You're coming here every Friday. . . . If you go Saturdays, she might not like it," said Auntie.

"I can ask her," I said. "She can only say no."

But she mustn't, I thought to myself. I need to go dancing too. Even with saving money and seeing the Lishofskys, I need to have my moments of fun.

"That's true," said Auntie, "but make sure you do. You don't want to anger her."

"Yes, Auntie, I will," I agreed. "Itkeh, why don't

you and Libeh come by tomorrow night. By then I will have spoken to Mrs. Goodman and I can tell you what she says."

"Whatever you say, Cousin," said Itkeh.

"But, Itkeh, make sure Fagel has spoken to her. Even though she stays there now, we're still responsible," Auntie said.

"I'm not a fool," said Itkeh.

"Don't talk back," said her mother.

Auntie pushed her chair back and held her big belly.

Uncle looked up.

"Maybe you should go lie down," he said.

"No," she said, "I'm fine."

"Soon we're going to have a baby," sang Rosie.

"I know," I said, ". . . and, Uncle, how is your new horse?"

"Ah, Fagel, thank you for asking. He's very good. I miss the old one, of course, but this new one can work harder."

"Better for all of us," said Auntie.

"Fagel," said Itkeh, finishing the last of the meat, "how come you've never had us over at your new house?"

"It's not my house."

"How can you ask that?" said Bessie.

"Why not? She comes here," said Itkeh.

"But we're her family. It's different. You can't go inviting yourself over to other people's houses," said Bessie.

"You'll see tomorrow," I said.

"Tell us about it," said Itkeh. "Where do you sleep?"

"In a bedroom," I answered.

"Who do you share it with?" asked Libeh.

"No one," I said.

"She's so fancy," said Itkeh. "She comes here and sleeps with us and then, all of a sudden, she gets to have her own room, like a rich girl."

"Enough," said Auntie. "She's not rich, she's a servant. Don't tease her."

"Mama," said Bessie, "you shouldn't say that."

"All right," said Auntie, "I take it back."

"Girls," said Uncle, "Fagel is a good girl to be saving for her family, just like Itkeh and Libeh, who give us their money."

"Have you been to the restaurant?" asked Sadie. "What's it like?"

"That's enough," said Auntie. "We're glad Fagel has a good job and can share our Sabbath, and meet us at synagogue. This way she stays with the family."

On my way back to the Goodmans, I calculated how much I was saving. Of the four dollars I got paid weekly, I could set aside two or three. I only needed to buy shoes or a present for Rosie or stamps for letters, or maybe a ribbon for my hair if I do go dancing. As for clothes, I could buy scraps and make my own.

I guess it takes about seventy, seventy-five dollars

to come here—thirty-five dollars for the boat trip, about twenty-five dollars to show the inspector (five of which he takes), and more while traveling.

So pretty soon I should have the money. If I had stayed at the Lishofskys and paid them half my salary, I never could have made it.

I think of this all the time.

The other day, Cabot locked himself in the bathroom and wouldn't come out. After ten minutes, I wanted to kick the door in, but instead I thought of all the money I was saving and how Blume would be here to help me soon. So I waited. What could happen to him in the bathroom? If there was an emergency, I could send for someone from the restaurant. I let more time pass and I went to get the pajamas I was making. I brought a chair into the hall and sat there sewing.

Then I heard Cabot say, "Fagel, are you there?"

"Yes," I answered.

"Why aren't you begging me to open the door?" he asked.

"Why should I beg you?" I answered.

"Because I've been in here a long time and I locked the door on you."

"Yes," I said, "you are locked in, also. Maybe you need to stay in there."

"But, Fagel," Cabot said, "don't you miss me? Don't you want me to come out?"

"Yes," I said. "And you will."

Stewart came out of his room, brought a chair and sat next to me. I sewed and he read his school-book. Soon the bathroom door opened.

"Here I am," said Cabot.

"Hello, Cabot," Stewart and I said.

He smiled and went and got a chair to sit with us.

So, I *am* earning my money.

CHAPTER *17*

When Itkeh and Libeh arrived on Saturday night, I was already in my dancing dress, with new ribbons in my hair.

"Mrs. Goodman," I said, "you know my cousins."

Itkeh said, "It's good of you to let Fagel go with us."

I winced.

"But, of course," said Mrs. Goodman. "She does a good job. Now, girls, how are your mother and father?"

"They're fine," said Itkeh.

"Mother's almost due," said Libeh.

"Ah, another baby in the house," said Mrs. Goodman.

Itkeh looked around the living room as if she was trying to recall it later.

"It's time to go," I said. "Good-bye."

Quickly I walked down the steps to the street, with Itkeh and Libeh following me.

On the streetcar into Boston, Itkeh couldn't stop talking about the Goodmans' house.

"What a way to live!" she said.

"Yes," agreed Libeh, "all those upholstered couches and chairs and a carved wooden rocking chair."

"And the velvet carpet," said Itkeh. "I even noticed some silver candlesticks and gold goblets on the table in the next room."

"It must be nice to be rich," said Libeh.

Inside the dance hall we hung up our coats. I made my way to the dance floor, where I loved watching all the couples moving.

"Let's dance," said Libeh.

As we waltzed, I looked around the room to see if I recognized any faces. Then I saw the one I was looking for. Herschel from Chelsea came over and interrupted us.

"Hello, Fagel," said Herschel. "I looked for you the past few weeks, but I didn't see you."

"I couldn't come," I said, "I was busy changing houses."

90

"Oh," he said, "what happened?"

"Don't tell anyone but I moved out of my aunt's house and into another place."

"What place?" he asked.

"Oh, the lady I work for."

"Why is that a secret?"

"You know."

"No, I don't."

"How can you live apart from relatives? It's shameful for everyone."

"Fagel," said Herschel emphatically, "didn't I tell you last time we met that here is different from the old country? The same rules don't apply. Here the first rule is survival."

I looked down.

"Would you like to dance?" Herschel asked.

"Oh, yes!" I said.

It was so much fun to be with him. I didn't feel uncomfortable anymore. Not only could I follow him, but I was relaxed enough to enjoy having his arm around me.

Herschel asked if I would like something to drink.

"Here, Fagel, this is for you," he said, handing me a cup.

"Thank you."

"So what have you been doing?" he asked.

I laughed.

"A lot."

"Tell me," he said.

I looked at him and felt I could trust him, so I began to talk, really talk, like I'm not able to do with anyone else here.

"I'm working for Mrs. Goodman, whose husband owns the bar-restaurant in Chelsea."

"Which one?"

"On the corner of Broadway near the movie theater."

"I know it. I've even been there. When my brother graduated from high school, my parents took all of us out for dinner. That's where we went."

"Did you like it?"

"Very good."

"Yes, I think so too. I've eaten there several times. Whenever Mrs. Goodman doesn't want to cook dinner or stay in the house, we just go downstairs to eat. All the people there know us too. It's nice."

"So what do you do for the Goodmans?" Herschel asked.

"I watch the two boys, Cabot and Stewart."

"What does Mrs. Goodman do when you watch them?"

"Different things. Sometimes she goes shopping or cooks or visits relatives."

"Doesn't she like to watch her boys?"

"Well, she has a hard time with them," I admitted.

"Why?"

"They don't listen to her."

"And they listen to you?"

"More and more," I smiled.

He laughed.

"How did you get them to listen to you?"

"Do you want to know the truth?"

"Yes," said Herschel, looking very serious.

"I made up my mind that they had to listen. I need the money and I don't want them to drive me crazy like they do their mother. I took care of all my younger brothers and sisters, so I had some idea what to do. When I felt like throwing something, I just said to myself Blume, Hatzkel, Nahamkah, Zelig, Herschel, Pinchas, Mamenyu. That quieted me down. Once they saw they couldn't drive me crazy, it got easier."

"Who are those people?"

"My family in Slonim I'm going to bring over."

"Well," said Herschel, "you must be proud of yourself."

"Yes," I admitted, "I already have ten dollars saved. I'm going to save the other sixty, sixty-five very quickly, two or more dollars a week. When I have enough, I will send my family a boat ticket and money to come."

"Now, Fagel," said Herschel, "before you send them the ticket or money, you must talk to me."

"Why?"

"Because there's a right way and a wrong way to do things. I've been in America longer than you, and I know who to ask. There are people who could cheat you. Don't go to strangers. You can rely on me."

"Thank you," I said, feeling suddenly shy.

I felt protected in a way I hadn't been since I left Slonim. He was like Hatzkel, or even Daddy.

"I want to see you again," said Herschel.

"Yes," I said.

I couldn't help but think of Daddy again. Meeting a boy who wasn't chosen or known by the family did not meet approval in the old country.

"When can we meet?"

"I don't know," I said. "I already asked Mrs. Goodman if I can go to Auntie's for Sabbath dinner and here tonight. I don't know when I can leave the house again."

"Well, do you go to synagogue Saturday mornings?"

"Yes," I admitted, "we do."

"Which one?" Herschel asked.

"Ayuda Achim."

I didn't care about what was done in the old country. I wanted to see Herschel again.

"I know where that is," he said. "Next Saturday when you go, I'll meet you after services and walk you back to Mrs. Goodman's."

"Yes," I agreed, smiling in spite of myself.

CHAPTER 18

Last night I went to my first night school class in America!

I spoke to Mrs. Goodman and asked if I could attend one night a week.

"Libeh and Itkeh go there," I said.

"Well, Fagel, you are wanting to leave the house a great deal. I need you to be with Cabot and Stewart, but how can I say no to your going to school? Every child should be in school. Can't you go during the day?"

I shook my head no.

"Why not?" she asked.

"Only little children go during the day. My older cousins go at night. They said there's a class that teaches English Wednesday nights, so I'd like to try that."

"Well, for now, all right, but we'll talk more about this later," she said.

That evening I went downstairs at seven o'clock and met Itkeh and Libeh. I didn't want them to come upstairs and bother the Goodmans again.

"So, Fagel," said Itkeh, "are you ready to go this time?"

"Yes," I said.

"No more greenhorn," said Itkeh. "You learn the right American words and you'll be just like everyone else in Chelsea."

"Yes," I said, "and then I can go shopping and talk to officials and bosses, in English too."

"Yes," said Libeh.

We had arrived at another school, just as official-looking as the one Auntie had brought me to. Sweat broke out on my forehead. Still, I waited at the counter until a businesslike woman waited on us.

"I want to register my cousin," Itkeh told the lady.

I was relieved to hear the woman speak Yiddish, our mother tongue.

The lady asked me some questions, put answers on a paper, then gave me another paper to take to my teacher.

"The class meets in three-oh-eight," she added.

"Thank you," I said.

Itkeh and Libeh walked me to the door of 308.

"We'll meet you downstairs in front of the office after class," said Itkeh.

"Can you find it?" asked Libeh.

"Yes," I said, not knowing if I could, but not wanting to appear stupid.

They hurried off to their classes and I opened the door. I walked up to a tall young woman wearing glasses, standing in front of a big desk, and handed her the paper. She examined it and said, "Fagel Fratrizsky," and then some English words.

I nodded yes.

She pointed to a chair.

Then she spoke some more English and a fat girl with tightly curled hair, sitting next to me, leaned over and said, in Yiddish, "I'll translate for you. The teacher only speaks English. If you don't understand something, tell me."

"Thank you."

I looked around the room. There were about twenty students. Most of them looked older than me. In fact, some were about Mother's age.

The teacher said something and all the students stood up and folded an arm across their chests. I got up too and put my arm the same way. Then the teacher turned around, looked at the flag at the front of the room, and spoke in unison with the students. Then together they sang a song in which I recognized the word *America*.

When everyone sat down, I leaned over and asked my translator what that was.

"That's the pledge to America."

I wasn't sure what that meant but thought I could ask Itkeh and Libeh later.

Then the students began to talk. They went around the room saying to the person next to them, "My name is Samuel"—or whatever their names were. . . . I couldn't remember all of them. "What is your name?"

I was nervous when they came to me, but I just tried to imitate what the others were saying.

Then the teacher held up a piece of chalk and said some more words. She called on each student to come to the front of the room, pick up the chalk, and say the same words that she had just said. I realized they were saying the same thing each time. Then, I could hear separate words.

The teacher pointed at me. Slowly I got up and took the chalk.

"I have a piece of chalk," the teacher said in English.

I guessed she was talking about the chalk.

"I have a piece of chalk," I tried to say.

The teacher repeated it again and again. I tried to copy her. After several tries, she said, "Good," and I happily returned to my seat.

Next the teacher went to the door, opened it, and said some more words beginning with *I*. She

pointed at different students who took turns opening the door and mimicking her.

"I open the door," my translator whispered.

That's what I had guessed!

When the teacher shut the door, I whispered
back, "I shut the door."

Using a slate, desk, and chair the teacher repeated
more words. By now I was beginning to catch on,
just as if I were learning words to a new melody.
It was fun.

"Now we say good-bye," the teacher had the class
say together. She made us repeat it until the *we*
didn't sound like *vee*.

I was happy. This class was not embarrassing. No
one else knew more than I did.

Itkeh and Libeh were waiting for me.

"So how was it?" said Itkeh.

"It was fine," I said.

"This time you didn't run away," she added.

I didn't answer. I was thinking about coming next
week. One night of school added to Sabbath with
the Lishofskys, Saturday night dancing, and more
free time for whatever else the New World offers
was a lot.

Isn't that what Mrs. Goodman would think?

_C_HAPTER _19_

Yesterday Mrs. Goodman and I were sitting in the living room. She was drinking her tea and I was finishing the hem on a pair of pants for Stewart.

"Fagel," she said, "I've been thinking about how many times you've been away from the house recently. I need you here in the evenings when the boys are home. Going to your family for Friday night dinner, I can understand. I can't deprive a young girl away from home from spending the Sabbath with her family. I certainly can't tell you not to go to school. But why do you have to go at night? Why can't you go in the day, like Stewart and Cabot do?"

"I already told you," I said, "my older cousins go in the evening."

"I know," said Mrs. Goodman, "but it doesn't make sense. They work during the day so they have to go at night, but other children your age attend school during the day. Why can't you?"

"But I'm not like those other children who already speak English," I answered.

"No," agreed Mrs. Goodman. "I agree you should be taking English classes, but I'm going to have to see if Chelsea schools don't have such classes during the day."

"All right," I said.

It wasn't all right. All I could think of was being put with little children and embarrassed. I didn't want to tell Mrs. Goodman that, so I just kept my head down, in my sewing.

"I have to go to the store," said Mrs. Goodman.

When she returned, I had almost finished the one cuff.

"Fagel," she said, "I ran into your aunt and she had this letter for you."

"Oh, thank you," I said.

I looked at the address. It was from Mother.

"Excuse me," I said, and went to my room to read.

November 16, 1907

Dear Fagel,

I hope this letter finds you well. Everyone sends you their love. We think of you all the time and wish you were here with us.

Zelig is doing better in cheder this year. Pinchas, of course, is constantly praised by his teacher. Blume makes fine hats. She's ready to be paid for her work. I'm still trying to decide whether to send Nahamkah to your old workshop with Mr. Antowicki. I like to have her around the house, but if you others have trades, shouldn't she? Herschel had a bad toothache, but we pulled the tooth and he's better.

Now, little Fagel, listen carefully. I'm proud of you, working hard at your new job and saving. You are doing the right thing and so are the Lishofskys, who were kind enough to take you in.

I told you before that you are to give them your money. They have taken care of you and they need it.

Like you, I want the family to stay together, but again I say I can't send the Lishofskys any more children.

The family in Argentina is good. They have opened a food store and can always use another person to help out. They kept asking me to send Blume. What could I tell them?

*Finally, I bought a ticket for her. She is set
to leave this month.*
Fagel, I wish it didn't have to be like this.
Love from all of us.

Your Mamenyu,
Shaneh Gittel

I put the letter in my second drawer, where I keep
all my things from home. As I did, I saw the picture
Nahamkah had given me. I looked at all of us again.
How could we ever have guessed that we would
live so far apart? I began to hum "Raizele."

I heard a knock at my bedroom door.

"Fagel," Mrs. Goodman said, "I need you to help
me prepare dinner."

"Coming," I said and put away my precious picture, after touching a finger to my lips and then to
the picture.

"Here," said Mrs. Goodman, "you peel and cut
up these onions while I start the soup."

I was glad it was onions, so if I began to cry, it
wouldn't look strange. But I didn't want to cry tears.
I wanted to cry out, "No, no, no, no, no. It's not
fair. Everything is going wrong."

"Fagel," Mrs. Goodman said loudly, "watch yourself. You almost cut your finger."

With effort, I made myself cut slower and more
carefully.

Cabot entered the room with a ball. He bounced
it on the floor.

"Can't you play with that someplace else?" said Mrs. Goodman. "You can see we're making dinner."

Cabot bounced his way out of the room.

When I finished the onions, Mrs. Goodman gave me some carrots and celery to chop.

Cabot reentered.

"What's for dinner?" he asked.

"Chicken," said Mrs. Goodman.

"How soon?" he asked.

"When it's ready," said Mrs. Goodman.

He looked at her and smiled. Then he pulled the chair away from the kitchen table and climbed up on it. He smiled wider this time.

"Look at me," he sang, "I'm the king of the castle."

He jumped to the floor. Then he climbed on the chair.

"Yes, I'm the king of the castle," he sang again.

"Stop that," said Mrs. Goodman.

"I can't," he said.

Again he jumped to the floor, climbed on the chair, jumped to the floor, climbed on the chair, and sang, "And you're a dirty rascal!"

"Stop that right now," Mrs. Goodman said.

Cabot paid no attention.

"Cabot, please," Mrs. Goodman pleaded.

"And you're the dirty rascal!"

Finally, I put my knife down, grabbed Cabot around the waist, and put him solidly on the floor. He stared at me and I stared back. Then he left the room.

"Fagel," said Mrs. Goodman, "you didn't have to be so rough."

I didn't answer.

"That was not necessary," said Mrs. Goodman.

I lowered my eyes to the ground.

"I can finish dinner by myself tonight. You can leave now, Fagel. I'll call you when it's ready."

I went to my room, every muscle in my body tightened. Now I know why people say it's bad to be a servant. Bosses think they own you and can tell you what to do all the time.

Oh, God, help me, please.

Don't let Mother send Blume away.

I feel like a fish caught in a net, trapped and trying to get out.

_C_HAPTER _20_

I couldn't figure out how I could sneak away from the Goodmans to meet Herschel after synagogue. While the rabbi was reading from the Torah, I finally did—I would ask Mrs. Goodman if I could visit with my cousins before going back to her house.

"I suppose so, Fagel," said Mrs. Goodman.

"Thank you," I said, and hurried off to be with the Lishofskys.

"Are you coming home with us, Fagel-bird, or will you fly away again?" Rosie asked.

"Not today," I said, watching the Goodmans make their way out of synagogue.

I said good-bye to the relatives and went outside. Herschel was waiting. He smiled and I smiled back.

"Would you like to go for a walk?" he asked.

"Yes," I said softly.

We walked toward Broadway. As we neared Chelsea Square, Herschel said, "Would you like something to drink?"

We walked to a little candy store with a counter, where we perched on stools.

"What do you want?" Herschel asked.

"I don't know," I said. "What do you get here?"

"Sodas."

He ordered and the man behind the counter brought us drinks in paper cups sitting in metal containers. I tasted mine . . . a bit bubbly but not bad.

"Do you like it?"

"Yes, thank you."

Herschel gave the man some coins and then I followed him out of the store to the triangular park called Chelsea Square. He sat down on a bench. I sat next to him.

"You haven't been there before?" Herschel asked.

"No."

"Where have you been?"

"Mostly I stay with Mrs. Goodman. I've been to the butcher and the food store."

"You're so sheltered," he said.

"I guess," I said. "What do you do?"

"I work in a laundry. I do the pressing and put the clothes on hangers. I work there full-time, six days a week. I make good money and I'm saving. I want to go into business for myself. I watch the price of everything—what the customer pays and how much supplies and labor cost. I can't tell how much money my boss takes home, but he lives nicely."

Once again I was impressed with Herschel. He was serious and responsible. He didn't seem like a stranger.

"Do you want to have your own laundry?" I asked.

"Why not?" he said. "At least, it's a business I know something about."

"Sounds like a good idea."

"It is a good idea," he agreed.

We sat silently for a while. It felt nice to be next to him like that.

"Well, Fagel," said Herschel, "what do you want to do?"

"I want to bring my family here," I said.

"I know," said Herschel.

"But, Herschel, now there's a problem," I said.

"What?" said Herschel.

"My mother is sending Blume to Argentina. The relatives there are asking for someone. Since I can't tell her that I don't have to give my money to Auntie and Uncle, she doesn't understand how much I have saved."

"Yes," said Herschel.

"Well, what do I do?"

"Tell her that you are paying off a ticket now while giving to the Lishofskys. It's true because you're not costing them anything now and you're saving a lot.

"Also, Fagel, whether you like it or not, she might send your sister to Argentina."

"Don't say that," I cried.

"Fagel," said Herschel.

"You can't say that. It was bad enough when my father died and I had to leave. We have to be reunited! That's why I'm working like a slave. Why else would I come here? Why else would I spend all day with someone hovering over me telling me what to do, minding two impossible little boys? Why?"

"Fagel," said Herschel, "I'm not trying to hurt you."

"I have a terrible, lonely life but all because I am going to finally have my family here. It's too hard to live without my family."

I paused.

Herschel touched my arm.

"Fagel," he said.

I wiped my eyes. I would not cry in public.

"Fagel," Herschel repeated, "I was only trying to say that we don't always get our wishes. Even if Blume isn't sent here, couldn't you send for another family member?"

I didn't like what he was saying.

"But I thought we'd all be together in the New World."

"I hope you can be."

"There's more," I said. "Mrs. Goodman doesn't like my leaving the house. She wants me to stay there all the time. Each time I want to do something, she makes me feel terrible."

"You're not a slave, Fagel. You're a worker and workers have rights too."

"You sound like my big brother, Hatzkel," I said.

I almost told him Hatzkel is my strong spruce.

"Well, it's true. Even people who live in get one day and one night off, usually the Sabbath."

"What did you ask for?"

"Friday night dinners with the cousins, Saturday dancing, and Wednesday I just started English classes. And I want to spend some time with Rosie."

"So you want two nights a week plus school?"

I nodded.

"That's not too much," he said. "Maybe you could get a half Saturday too. You should have talked about this when you agreed to work for her, but I guess you didn't know."

"No, I didn't."

"Has Mrs. Goodman ever had a live-in before?"

"I don't think so."

"Maybe she doesn't know. You have to tell her."

"How?"

"You just say, 'I have talked to other people. They say everyone who works my job gets this much time off. I should too.' "

"What if she fires me?"

"She won't. And if she does, you can get another job."

"How?"

"Your cousins or I will find you one. Maybe it'll be better."

I shook my head.

"Sometimes you say frightening things, Herschel."

"I'm only trying to help."

"Yes, but you forgot about school."

"No," he said, "I didn't. She has to let you go to school. If she can find a good day class, you'll go then. If not, you will go at night."

"But I don't want to be with little children."

"Not with little children, but with big children during the day. If she can't find that, she'll have to let you go at night."

"You make it sound so easy."

"Fagel," said Herschel, "it's not easy, but it's your life. You're not a slave and you can send for your family."

I just sat still.

"Remember when I met you and said you were courageous? Now," said Herschel, "is exactly when you need that courage."

I nodded.

CHAPTER *21*

The next day, I kept thinking about what Herschel said. I hoped he was wrong about Blume but right about my days off. I had to talk to Mrs. Goodman. I waited until the boys were playing nicely and asked her if we could speak.

"All right, Fagel," she said.

I followed her into the living room, where I sat in a chair across from her.

"What is it?" she asked.

"Well, Mrs. Goodman, I've been talking to a few people and they say that people who work jobs like mine, where they live in and help out with the

113

family, well, that people like that get one whole day without work. See, what I mean, is that they know before they start working that they won't have to come to work from Friday night until Saturday night."

"What people say this?" asked Mrs. Goodman.

"People, just people I know," I said.

"I see," said Mrs. Goodman.

"I know I should have spoken to you about this before I started working, but I didn't know then, so I'm thinking now that we should agree on half of Saturday, Friday and Saturday nights, regular, which I would have to myself and not be here," I said, all out of breath.

Mrs. Goodman thought for a while.

"Fagel," she said, "may I ask you a question?"

"Of course," I said.

"Do you think I treat you badly?"

"No."

"Do you want to continue to work here?"

"Yes," I said, "I do. I want to work for you."

"Well," she said, "I have to think about this. It sounds like a lot of time away from here. Let me speak to Mr. Goodman. He hires a lot of employees and he'll know."

There was a knock at the door.

"Thank you," I said.

"You're welcome," she answered, and went to open the door.

114

Bessie was standing there. Both Mrs. Goodman and I were surprised to see her.

"Why, hello," said Mrs. Goodman. "Please come in."

"Hello, Mrs. Goodman," she said, "I'm Bessie Lishofsky. I don't know if you know me."

"Certainly," said Mrs. Goodman, "I know you from synagogue. Please sit down."

"Thank you," said Bessie, "but I can't sit. I just came to tell you that my mother's having the baby."

"Oh, Bessie," said Mrs. Goodman, "how wonderful. Fagel, put some coats on the boys and we'll all go over.

"And Fagel, go into the kitchen and see what we have prepared. Take whatever is there. Put it in a basket to bring with us. Hurry."

Bessie threw her arms around me.

"I'm so excited," she said.

"Come," I said, "help me get the food."

We walked past the dining room with its polished, dark wood dining table, and into the kitchen, where the pots and pans shone on the shelf.

"Itkeh had told me this was a nice house," Bessie said.

"They live well," I agreed.

I wrapped up the leftover chicken, vegetables in jars, chicken liver, and two breads, and put them in the basket.

115

"Isn't she nice?" said Bessie.

"Yes," I agreed, "when she's not being bossy."

Mrs. Goodman appeared at the kitchen door with Cabot and Stewart.

"Watch the boys while I get one more thing," she said.

She opened the lower door of the armoire and took out a bottle of wine.

"A celebration calls for something special," she said.

We left the house.

"So how is your mother doing?" Mrs. Goodman asked.

"Fine, so far," said Bessie.

"And the midwife?" asked Mrs. Goodman.

"She's already there."

"Hurrah," said Cabot, "there's going to be a baby."

We rushed up the stairs. When we opened the door, I saw relatives I now knew well seated around the kitchen.

I put the basket on the table.

"This is Mrs. Goodman and her boys, Cabot and Stewart. She brought some food and wine to celebrate."

"Hello," said Mrs. Goodman. "Where is she?"

"I'll take you," said Bessie.

"Fagel, watch the boys," said Mrs. Goodman before going down the hall.

Three relatives got up and offered us their chairs.

"Sit down," I told Auntie's brother. "I'm a relative. I don't need special treatment."

Then I told Cabot and Stewart to sit. They must have noticed the seriousness in my voice, because they sat very still.

The relatives continued to talk and eat. I gave Cabot and Stewart a plate of chicken, potatoes, and carrots.

We all waited.

Steps came down the hall. It was Rosie!

"Rosie," I cried.

She ran over and we hugged happily.

More steps came down the hall. Everyone turned to see who it was.

Itkeh announced, "It's a boy!"

"Mazel tov, congratulations!" Everyone screamed, and began hugging and kissing each other.

Auntie's brother opened a bottle of whiskey and poured as many glasses as he could find. This was a time to celebrate, just like a holiday.

"A toast," he said, "L'chayim. To life."

"A boy," said his wife. "Whoever thought there would be a son in this family."

Uncle came rushing into the room.

"I have a son!" he shouted.

Itkeh handed him a glass. He raised it high in the air.

"Blessed art thou, Lord our God, King of the Universe, who has kept us alive and brought us to this moment," he sang.

"May the evil eye spare the little one," said Auntie's brother.

Uncle hugged Itkeh on one side and Rosie on the other.

Everyone drank some more.

It was quite something!

*C*HAPTER *22*

Sometimes Mrs. Goodman makes me mad. The boys are getting easier to be with but she gets more demanding all the time.

Yesterday she decided that it was time to see about a day school for me.

"Fagel," she said in that too proper way she has of speaking Yiddish, as if she were American and didn't come from the old country like everyone else, "I want you to come with me to Shurtloff School. If they have English classes during the day, you can go with the boys."

"Fine," I said.

But it wasn't fine. How dare she try to put a girl going on fourteen in a babies' school!

On the way over, I kept my lips together so they wouldn't say something they shouldn't.

When we got to the school door, I stopped.

"We're going to go to the office to speak to the secretary," she said.

"I'll wait outside," I answered.

"Why?" she asked.

"I want to," I said.

"But it will only be a minute," she said. "Then you can decide what to do."

"I know what I want to do," I said, "wait here."

She looked at me closely.

"Sometimes, Fagel," she said, "I just don't understand you."

I understood her all too well. She wanted to own me.

"Well, all right, I'll go by myself," she said, and entered the building.

I felt proud of myself. I don't care if she fires me. I can get another job. She can't tell me what to do.

When she came out, she said, "They do have classes during the day for children six to fifteen years old. I'll let you decide. I spoke to Mr. Goodman"—why does she always refer to her own husband as Mr. Goodman? Doesn't he have a first name?—"and he said that if you want to have three nights, you can't have another half-day. If you take two nights, you can have half Saturday."

He said...he said...If you want a half, take a quarter. If you want a quarter, take nothing.

"Thank you," I said.

"Fagel," she said, "I don't want to lose you. I like having you around the house. So do the boys and Mr. Goodman. It's like you're my daughter."

Enough, I thought. For sure, I am not your daughter. Then I had an idea.

"Mrs. Goodman," I said, "we haven't seen my aunt since the baby was born. Can we visit her?"

"What a good idea, Fagel. Let's stop and pick up some challah and bagels."

We went to the nearest bakery, where it took her a long time to choose between breads and make the decision whether to slice it or not.

Soon we were walking up the familiar stairs. I was looking forward to seeing Auntie—my real family, not a pretend one.

Mrs. Goodman knocked.

Auntie, looking very tired, opened the door.

On the stove was the boiling water with clothes. In her arms was a crying baby.

"Fagel," said Auntie, "what a nice surprise. Come in, Mrs. Goodman, excuse the mess. You know how it is when babies come."

"Oh, yes, I do, Mrs. Lishofsky," said Mrs. Goodman. "What a sweet little boy."

She took him from Auntie's arms.

He cried louder.

"What's his name?" asked Mrs. Goodman.

121

"Baruch," said Auntie. "It's a blessing for us to have a boy, finally."

"Girls are nice too," said Mrs. Goodman. "I've always wanted one."

"Well, I've got many more than one," said Auntie, "and now I've got a boy, thank God. When my husband and I leave this earth, he'll say prayers for us. He'll keep our name alive."

Mrs. Goodman grasped Baruch tightly and walked around with him. He screamed louder.

"Would you like some tea?" asked Auntie.

"Please," said Mrs. Goodman, "that is, if it's no trouble."

"How much trouble is putting water on to boil?"

"Thank you, Mrs. Lishofsky."

Auntie went to the stove, moved the clothes pot to the side, and added the tea kettle next to it.

Mrs. Goodman had finally gotten Baruch to quiet down. She seemed so absorbed in rocking him, that it was almost as if Auntie and I were alone, like we used to be.

"Fagel," Auntie said, as I stood next to her.

"Yes?"

"I got a letter from your mother."

"Yes," I waited.

"She thanks us for taking such good care of you and wanted to know if you were really making as much money as you said and if you were giving us some."

I waited.

122

"I haven't answered her yet."

Auntie paused. She took the cups down from the top shelf.

"But I'm going to tell her it's all true. After all, it is, isn't it?"

"Sort of," I said.

"That's what I mean," she said.

She took down her teapot and filled it with some black Russian tea leaves. Then she put some cookies on a plate.

"Here, Fagel, take the cups to the table."

Auntie brought the cookies.

"I miss you, little one," she said.

"I miss you too," I admitted.

"There's no one here all day to listen to me complain."

"You didn't complain so much."

"Enough. I complain enough. It's good not to keep things on your chest."

"I'm going to school, Auntie."

"Yes," she said, pouring the boiling water over the tea leaves. "Itkeh and Libeh told me. I'm proud of you. I always knew you would. Remember that day when you ran out of Cary School?"

I nodded my head.

"You were so scared someone would come and get you. This isn't Russia . . . no pogroms, no drunken people beating us up. I'm not saying life is easy. But it is a *life*, not just a wait for death. That's something."

"Auntie, I've saved twenty-three dollars already."

"Very good. I expect we should be seeing another Fratrizsky soon."

"Oh, Auntie, I hope so, but Mother is sending Blume to Argentina."

"Argentina . . . ," said Auntie. "She should come here."

"Of course. Could you tell my mother that?"

"I could."

"Then we could keep our family together."

"God willing."

CHAPTER 23

I got Mother's letter yesterday. I read it over and over. I couldn't believe it then and I can't believe it now. Blume has left. Now Mother wants to send Zelig, because he wants to work in the store too. I'm like a sleepwalker; nothing seems real.

I wasn't even excited when Mr. Goodman said he had a wonderful surprise for us. We got dressed for the cold weather and went downstairs. There stood an automobile with a driver, waiting to take us for a ride.

I'd never been in an automobile before. Neither had Cabot nor Stewart. They started bouncing up and down in the backseat next to me. I felt sick. Finally their father told them to stop and they quieted down and just looked out the window.

It was fun to see streets whizzing by, as if we were on a train. Just as a house came into view, off it went, like you couldn't hold onto anything too long.

"Look at that dog," screamed Cabot.

"Where?" said Stewart.

Cabot pointed and as soon as you followed his finger with your eye, the dog was already left behind.

Mr. Goodman acted like he was captain of the ship, sure and in charge. He pointed out places he knew, mostly restaurants and bars he had visited.

Mrs. Goodman sat next to him in the front seat, with a little smile on her face. She barely spoke but sat very straight, as if everyone we passed could see she was a woman whose husband had hired a car.

We kept driving and driving. Pretty soon there were few houses and much more land without people. We passed a few farms and many, many trees.

Then Mr. Goodman ordered the driver to pull to the side of the road and stop.

"Mrs. Goodman, children," he said, "I know it's too cold for a picnic, but we can still walk."

"Boo," said Cabot.

"Now, Cabot," said Mr. Goodman, "that's enough. You're dressed warmly enough, and once we start, you'll warm up even more. Fresh air is good for you.

"If you're good, we'll stop at my friend's restaurant on the way back."

"Hurrah," said Cabot.

"We'll be good," said Stewart.

Mr. Goodman led the way into the trees. Out of habit, I took Cabot's hand as we followed him.

"One, two, three, four, we are going off to war," sang Mr. Goodman at the top of his voice.

"Five, six, seven, eight, we are going to celebrate."

Mr. Goodman took large steps, beating his chest as he moved.

"Come on, now, boys, march. This is healthy for you."

The boys rushed to keep up with him.

"And sing with me," he began again. "One, two, three, four, we are going off to war."

Cabot and Stewart got the numbers right and half the other words too.

"Five, six, seven, eight, we are going to celebrate."

This time, Cabot and Stewart sang louder.

Silently I sang "Raizele."

It was a happy family scene, but not for me. The last time I was in the woods was with Mother in Slonim, and while this was not our woods, there were trees. There was a pine that looked like the silly Zelig pine in Slonim. Then there was a tall oak that could have passed for Daddy's stately tree... and a spruce that was almost as sturdy as the Hatzkel spruce, and a linden that spread its sheltering arms like Mamenyu's.

"One, two, three, four, we are going off..."

Tears started to fill my eyes.

"Five, six, seven, eight, we are..."

I wished I was alone and could hug the spruce that was almost a Hatzkel spruce or talk to the sheltering linden and ask Mamenyu why she sent Blume so far away from us.

We came into a large clearing ringed by a grove of fruit trees, but since it was winter, there were no fruits or flowers or leaves on the trees. Only the bare silhouettes rose against the sky.

The brisk air whistled through my coat.

"One, two, three..."

And then I saw a black cherry tree, its stark branches reaching upward. No white flowers like my Blume tree wore last July in Slonim. No black-purple fruit to crush against your teeth and drop sweetness in your mouth, and most of all, no Blume... no Blume ever to be here with me in this Chelsea.

I began to cry.

"Fagel," said Mrs. Goodman, "what is it?"

"Nothing," I said.

"Nobody cries over nothing," said Mrs. Goodman.

Cabot dropped my hand, reached up and put his hand on my shoulder.

"Poor Fagel," he said, "she's crying."

"So?" said Mr. Goodman.

"Some of these trees remind me of our woods in Slonim," I said.

"That's not a reason to cry," said Mr. Goodman.

I began to cry even more.

"You talk to her," said Mr. Goodman to his wife.

"Fagel," she said, "stop it now."

"But I won't see them again," I said, "and now my sister's being sent away."

"Things could be worse," said Mrs. Goodman. "You're lucky you have so many brothers and sisters. I am an only child and Mr. Goodman's brother lives far away. And you have a good job with good people, us."

"Yes," I nodded.

"Good-bye, sister," said Cabot. "What's her name?"

"Blume."

"Good-bye, Blume," said Cabot.

"Good-bye, Blume," said Stewart.

I turned around and started to walk back to the automobile.

"Where are you going?" asked Mrs. Goodman.

"I'm ready to go home," I said. "I'm through with the trees."

"Well, we're not ready to go," said Mrs. Goodman, "until my husband says so."

"All right," said Mr. Goodman, "let's find our restaurant."

"Hurrah," said Cabot. "Good-bye trees."

"Good-bye trees," said Stewart.

I turned around and gave one last look.

"Good-bye trees," I echoed.

CHAPTER 24

When Itkeh and Libeh came to take me dancing, I couldn't find my money. I had looked all over my room. I always put my money in the third drawer of my dresser. It wasn't there. I had looked in the other drawers and through my clothes but I couldn't find it. I had looked all around the room, under the bed. I had pulled apart the bed and looked on and in the desk. I still couldn't find it.

As soon as the cousins entered, I said, "I can't find my money."

"Do you want me to look for you?" Itkeh asked.

"Yes," I said.

Itkeh and Libeh followed me to my bedroom.

"I usually put it in an envelope here," I said, opening the drawer.

Itkeh looked through the drawers. Libeh looked around the room.

"It's not here," said Libeh.

"It's not in the drawers," said Itkeh.

"Oh no," I cried, "what do I do? I've already saved thirty-five dollars and now what do I do?"

"There's nothing to do," said Itkeh. "Either you can stay here and keep looking for it, or come dancing with us and we'll pay for you. You can pay us back later."

"How can I pay you back if I have no money?"

"You'll pay us back from your next week's wages."

"I can't just lose thirty-five dollars! How can I send for my family? How can I keep my family together? How can I send a ticket for Blume?"

"Well," said Itkeh, "it will turn up. Probably it's someplace you forgot you put it."

I started to cry.

"What will I do? I'm so far away, and if I lose the money, I'll never be able to see my family again."

Libeh put her arms around me.

"Don't worry, Fagel," she said, "it will turn up."

Itkeh sat down on my bed and waited. Finally she

132

said, "Look, Fagel, I'm sorry you can't find your money, but tonight is Saturday and we want to go dancing. You can stay here or go with us."

"I can't stay alone," I said. "I'll be too crazy."

"So where are the Goodmans?" she asked.

"They're at the restaurant."

"You can join them there."

"No!" I said.

I sat down. Libeh sat down on the bed next to Itkeh.

"So decide, Fagel," said Itkeh. "I'll give you five minutes."

My head was spinning. I had to have my money. I just had to, but I didn't know what to do anymore. I didn't want to stay alone or go to the restaurant.

"So Fagel?" said Itkeh.

"I'll go with you," I said.

I got my coat and turned out the light.

We climbed aboard the streetcar.

At the door, Itkeh paid for me.

Inside I remembered to hang up my coat. As I watched the boys and girls dancing around the room, it seemed like they were moving too fast and the music was too loud.

What I needed was a

"Whistle, and then call,
Come out, dear, come out!"

Someone tapped me on the shoulder.

"Where have you been?" Herschel said, "I've been looking for you a long time."

"I lost my money," I said.

"What?"

"I couldn't find it."

"So why are you here?"

I explained the whole story, and he said, "Let's go back and find it."

"Now?"

"You're not going to have any fun here. You'll just be worrying about it."

"Yes," I said, "let me talk to Itkeh."

"What is it?" she asked.

"Herschel is coming with me to look for the money."

"What?" said Itkeh. "He can't do that."

"Why not?"

"Because there's no one at the Goodmans'. You can't be alone with him. What will people say?"

"But Itkeh," I said, "he's a nice boy and he wants to help me."

"How do you know?" she asked. "Alone is different from public. I say you can't go."

She sounded like my father. I couldn't listen to those voices. I was in the New World. It was time to decide for myself.

"I'm going," I said.

"Fagel," she yelled.

I turned around. "Yes?"

"Do me a favor. Stop by the restaurant and tell the Goodmans what happened—if they're not back in the house. If you don't go into the empty house with him, I give you my permission."

Herschel and I walked to the trolley. All the way there, we didn't talk. Herschel had to nudge me when our stop came.

We walked to the restaurant in silence, and the barman told us the Goodmans had gone home.

"They're upstairs," I told Herschel. "Follow me."

I led him up the stairs and into the house.

Mrs. Goodman was sitting in the living room, next to a huge heart-shaped box of brightly wrapped chocolates.

"Oh, Fagel," she said, "you surprised me."

"Mrs. Goodman, I want you to meet my friend, Herschel. He's here because I couldn't find my money and he offered to help me look for it."

"Oh," said Mrs. Goodman.

Herschel and I stood. No one spoke. Mrs. Goodman didn't even ask him to sit down.

Finally Herschel said, "Well, I should be going. I think you can help Fagel find her money. Nice to meet you. Good-bye, Fagel. See you soon."

Then he walked out the door.

I was furious. Couldn't she even be polite enough to say hello to him? I started to go to my bedroom when Mrs. Goodman, looking up from unwrapping a chocolate, spoke.

"Fagel, you know you shouldn't be bringing strange boys to my house."

"Mrs. Goodman, he's not a stranger. He's my friend."

"From that place where you dance?"

"A friend is a friend."

"This is my house and I decide who comes here or not."

"But this was an emergency."

"What emergency?" she asked, unwrapping still another chocolate, one with creme in the center.

"I can't find all the money I saved."

"So," said Mrs. Goodman, popping the candy into her mouth. Her eyes closed in satisfaction, and she continued.

"It's not as if you don't have a job. We pay you well too. See what a lucky girl you are. In only a short time, you'll earn back the money you lost and more. How much did you lose?"

"Thirty-five dollars," I admitted, "enough to buy a ticket for my sister or brother to come here."

"Thirty-five dollars," said Mrs. Goodman. "That's nothing to be upset about."

If I lost another family member to Argentina or someplace else, I'd never forgive myself.

"Here," said Mrs. Goodman, handing me a candy. "Take one. Eat it and you'll forget such a silly thing as losing money."

I took the chocolate and put it in my mouth. It tasted bitter.

136

"Good," said Mrs. Goodman. "Isn't that better? Have another. Now go to sleep and think sweet thoughts. In the morning, you won't even remember what happened."

I started to leave.

"Fagel, come back. I have something for you."

She dangled an envelope in front of me.

"My money!"

"All except the five dollars I took to teach you a lesson. You can't go leaving money lying on the floor. You're lucky I found it. You might have lost it all."

"But, now, I can't buy a ticket."

"In a few weeks you can, and this way you'll remember to take better care of it."

As I entered my bedroom, I threw the chocolate into the wastebasket. I wished it were Mrs. Goodman.

_C_HAPTER _25_

I fell into a deep sleep and had a dream so vivid, it seemed like I was living it. Well, it wasn't a dream, it was a nightmare.

I was walking up a hill, not a mountain, just a little hill. If I could only go a little farther up the hill and reach the top, I could start down the other side. On the other side were Pinchas, Zelig, Herschel, Hatzkel, Nahamkah, Blume, Mother, even Father, our mill house, our Szczara, and all of Slonim. The hillside was filled with sweet spring flowers. The ground was soft and easy to walk on. But I couldn't make it to the top and down the other side.

If only I could have walked a little faster, a little farther, I should have been able to make it easily. But I didn't. I woke up, sweating as if it were summer.

Little did I think, that day in the woods when Mother and I went for a walk and she asked me to seriously consider my decision, that I would feel so lonely, even surrounded by people.

My bones ache for my family.

I keep hearing the voice of my father.

Only one time did he ever get angry at me. He didn't lay a hand on me. He just kept repeating, how could you, my little Fagel-bird?

Near our mill house, there is a Christian cemetery where officers are buried. A whole orchestra comes out to bid them farewell. Lots of people march behind the big band playing patriotic tunes. Secretly I would follow them. I wouldn't listen to their priest or even sing the words, of course, but I couldn't resist such fine music so nearby.

One day Father saw me. He motioned with his hand for me to come. We walked in silence back to the mill. My eyes were focused on the ground. I felt so embarrassed. In his office, with no one else there, he said, "Fagel, how could you? After all our Jewish people have suffered, are you leaving me and the family to follow them? How could you?"

He shook his head and almost cried.

Finally, when I dared look up, I told him that I was only listening to music.

Then he raised his voice.

"Only music! We Jews have music too. No! I saw you following them—listening to them—acting as if you didn't belong to us. How could you?"

I began to cry. Instead of hugging me, as he usually did when I cried, he walked out of the mill. I didn't see him for the rest of the day.

After that, he never mentioned it, and returned to being the loving father we lost over three years ago.

Now my ears keep repeating: "How could you? As if you didn't belong to us..."

And I wonder, who do I belong to?

Am I still a Fratrizsky from Slonim?

If not, who am I?

_C_HAPTER _26_

Monday morning, I'm not even sure why, I began to pack. I folded all my clothes and put them on the bed. I didn't stop until everything I owned was shut tight inside that trunk. Then I pulled it toward the front of the room, and went into the kitchen.

"Good morning, Fagel," Mrs. Goodman said. "Feeling better today?"

My face made an expression like a smile.

"Well, Fagel," said Mrs. Goodman, "we're all alone. Stewart and Cabot have gone to school and even Mr. Goodman went off early today."

"Good," I said. "I have something to say."

"Can't it wait until we finish the breakfast dishes?"

"No," I said. "It can't wait. Mrs. Goodman, I'm leaving."

"What?" she said.

"I won't be working for you anymore. I'm already packed and I'll come back later to get my trunk, but I'm leaving your house now."

"What?" she repeated. "How can you leave? You have a job here."

"Yes," I agreed. "I used to work for you but not anymore."

"You can't just leave like that. What am I going to do without you? Who will take care of my boys and help me around the house?"

"I don't know. You'll have to figure that out yourself."

"But you have to tell me far enough in advance that I have time to find another person. That's the way it's done. Mr. Goodman told me."

"Mrs. Goodman, if you had treated me with the respect I deserve, I would have stayed until you found someone else, but you didn't. You treated me like a slave you can order around who has no rights of her own. But I'm not a slave, I'm a worker. I'm a trained worker who deserves the same rights any worker gets—regular hours, time off, regular duties, a place to bring my friends—"

142

"But you're more like a member of the family than a worker."

"I'm not a member of your family, and if I were, I'd expect more kindness. I'm not a slave. I'm not a serving girl. I'm not some poor relation. I'm a person who came to do a job for you and I did a good job and should have been treated well."

"Fagel, I don't understand what you're saying. You're talking like those employees who carry signs on the street saying the boss is no good to them. What is this? Are you a radical? Why didn't you tell me before?"

"No, Mrs. Goodman, I'm not a radical and I've never carried a picket sign. I'm just a person who works for her living. And I want to be treated that way."

"Fagel, you're upset about your money. This will pass. Stay for this week, at least."

"I can't," I said. "Good-bye."

I walked out the door and hurried down Broadway. Really I was a little crazy. I didn't know what I was doing. I just had to be away. I didn't know what I should do . . . go back to my cousins, or room somewhere else, or what . . .

But as I walked, I smiled.

I was free. No one owned me.

I walked to the laundry where Herschel worked and up to the counter. He was off on the side, pressing pants. When I caught his eye, he stopped his machine and came over.

"What are you doing here?" Herschel asked.

"I left the Goodmans," I said.

"Wait here," he said, "I'll speak to my boss and see if I can take my lunch early today."

I felt better. I knew Herschel would help me.

CHAPTER 27

So Herschel took my arm and led me out of his store.

"The boss said I could go now, but I don't have much time. What happened?"

"I left the Goodmans. I'm not going back to work for them anymore."

"Why?"

"I'm sick of being treated as less than a person. Mrs. Goodman took my money to teach me a lesson."

"She told you? Did she give it back?"

"She kept five dollars."

"Of your money? That thief! Where are you going to stay? How will you support yourself?"

"I'm not worried about that now. You told me that you or my cousins could get me a job and that there are many places to stay, here in the New World."

"Yes, I did. I only have a short time before I go back to work. What do you want to do right now?"

"See the man who sells passage tickets."

Past the laundry where he worked, on the second floor above the shoe store, Herschel knocked on the door.

"Come in," said a bent-over old man with a gray beard, dressed in a faded black suit. He locked the door after us.

We walked back to his desk, piled high with papers, and took chairs across from him.

"Let's see how much money you brought," the man said.

"Here is thirty dollars, first payment for a ticket from Bremen to New York, or Boston if you can," I told him.

"New York," said the man, "that's where the boat docks."

He opened his drawer and took out a form on which he wrote. Then he looked up.

"Name?" he said.

"Fagel," I said.

"And the name that goes on the ticket?" he asked.

"Hatzkel Fratrizsky."

He didn't ask me to spell it. He knew Russian-Jewish names.

When he finished writing, he said, "Now you owe me five dollars. Whenever you're ready, bring me the next payment. Everyone buys on installment here. We also have banking services where you can leave your money or borrow on credit."

"Thank you," I said.

He let us out, locking the door behind us again.

When we were downstairs, I said, "Oh, Herschel, I can hardly wait until my brother is here and I will no longer be alone."

"Yes," said Herschel, "but you're not alone now. You have the Lishofskys. You even got Stewart and Cabot to like you."

"It's not the same as my real family, starting with my big brother who looks after me."

We had arrived at Broadway.

"But you have me too," said Herschel. "Aren't I your friend?"

"Yes, Herschel, you are a good friend, and I appreciate all you have done for me."

"Thank you. I appreciate you too," said Herschel.

As we were walking, I stopped.

"Herschel," I said, "do you have a little more time?"

"Just a little," he said. "Why?"

"There's something I want to do."

I turned the other way and took a sharp left at the corner. We continued in that direction.

"Fagel, where are you taking me?" Herschel asked.

"You know," I said.

"You're going down to the water, but why? There's nothing to see there."

"Wait. You'll see."

"I've seen and it's all factories."

We kept walking.

"It's cold near the water too," said Herschel.

We had reached the edge of Chelsea, the water that divided it from Boston across the way.

"You think we're at Revere Beach?"

"No, it's just water. I wanted to see the ocean that goes into Boston Harbor and travels to New York—that I sailed on and Hatzkel will too."

"Crazy."

"Water is always moving," I said. "Watch it."

"You can barely see it. All I see are factories with people inside working . . . like I should be."

"Well, I can see the water and it's moving like it always does because it's always traveling, coming from here to there, sending people from one place to another."

"That's why they put the factories on the water, so they can ship as soon as the products are made."

"Look at that water. Soon it will be bringing my brother and my whole family here."

Herschel shook his head.

148

I walked to the edge of the water. Herschel waited near the factory door.

I looked back at him. We smiled at each other.

Then, instead of seeing Chelsea's calm harbor, I pictured the waves.

Forward they rolled, then back.

Forward they rolled, then back.

Once again they beat against a heart that wanted to stop.

Oh, how I wished I could have sent the ticket today.

Oh, how I wished Blume hadn't gone to Argentina.

Oh, how I wished Daddy were alive and here to be with us.

Forward went the waves, then back.

Forward went the waves, then back.

Forward, forward, forward.

Like them, I couldn't stop moving. What's gone is gone. I almost had the ticket. Soon I will. With Herschel and the Lishofskys' help, I will get a better job.

Forward you go.

You can't go back.

Though our majestic oak, Daddy, is planted firmly with God, and our flowering cherry, Blume, now grows in South America, my spruce, Hatzkel, and our sapling, Herschel, and our curving pine, Zelig, and our upright tamarack, Pinchas, and our delicate dogwood, Nahamkah, and our sheltering linden,

Mamenyu, will be carefully replanted here in American soil.

I am a wave, strong and flowing, carrying my loved ones here.